Another Time/Another Land

Another Time/Another Land

A Fictional Memoir

Robert M. Grossman

Library of Congress Control Number: 2011905989

ISBN:	Hardcover	978-1-4628-5524-7
	Softcover	978-1-4628-5523-0
	Ebook	978-1-4628-5525-4

This is a work of fiction. Names, characters, places and incidents either are the product of the author's imagination or are used fictitiously, and any resemblance to any actual persons, living or dead, events, or locales is entirely coincidental.

This book was printed in the United States of America.

To order additional copies of this book, contact:

Xlibris Corporation

1-888-795-4274

www.Xlibris.com

Orders@Xlibris.com

92967

Chapter 1

It was late in the afternoon when the plane carrying Ensign S. Paul Miner landed near Sidi Abdallah on the outskirts of Casablanca. He boarded the waiting bus and sat alone by the window. The driver announced that the bus would not be leaving for at least a half hour because it had to await the arrival of another plane with more naval officers who were also heading for the base at Port Lyautey.

As Paul peered out the window, his mind wandered back to his only other naval venture outside the United States. It had been his midshipmen cruise the summer before, and he hoped his upcoming two-year stint in Morocco would be as memorable as those six weeks in the Caribbean and particularly the time in Cuba.

He remembered that full moon over Guantanamo Bay and the immense darkness ornamented with stars everywhere he looked as he stood on the deck of the guided missile cruiser anchored in the stillness of the harbor. The Korean War had come to an uneasy closure that year, and, unbeknown to much of the world then, Castro was planning his revolution somewhere in the Cuban hills.

Earlier in the day, Paul and his midshipmen colleagues had been given a tour of the base, which kept being referred to as "Gitmo." It was an enormously impressive fortress with its sleek airfields, its array of antiaircraft weaponry, its regimented and impeccably dressed marines, and the availability at the exchange store of an abundance of inexpensive and delicious Cuban cigars.

The cruiser had anchored in the harbor off Havana the day before after being at sea for nearly a week. The midshipmen were told that they could spend the day sightseeing ashore but had to be back aboard ship by nine that night. They descended from the cruiser's deck into small boats. As they arrived at dockside, there were some thirty taxis waiting for them. When Paul and three of his buddies were ushered into one of the taxis, they instructed the driver to take them to where Papa Hemingway lived. The taxi driver looked puzzled as Paul kept saying "Hemingway, Hemingway," assuming he would finally figure it out. He was wrong. Along with all the other taxis, they were taken straight to the whorehouse section.

As long as they were there, they decided to inspect. They went from whorehouse to whorehouse, not to do business but just to gaze at what for Paul and many of the other midshipmen was their first exposure to the allure of another side to life. They had been given a lecture and shown a film aboard ship on gonorrhea and syphilis, and this was very much on their minds during the house-to-house promenade. When their tour ended, they got back in their waiting taxi and repeated Hemingway's name. This time they were whisked to a cockfight. After that, as the driver continued to question their Hemingway entreaties, he drove them straight to the Club San Francisco. There they were transfixed by the sight of near-naked women suspended trapeze-like from crystal chandeliers hanging from the gigantic, domed ceiling. They never did get to Hemingway's abode, but they rationalized that missed experience by assuming he wouldn't have agreed to see them anyway.

Paul put his Cuban reminiscences aside as the bus finally began to fill with the second planeload of naval officers. It pulled out of the airport and onto a narrow two-lane highway. There was still enough light for Paul to see dried-clay mosques with their domed roofs coming into view in the distance. Even though he had not had much sleep on the long flight, the allure of observing droves of Arabs on the side of the road kept him quite awake. Most of the Arab men wore garments of sackcloth, often with hoods, as they trudged along on their sandaled feet. Some were pulling donkeys laden with grain. Others led camels packed with cruses of oil, honey, and flax. Many of the women were covered in a darkened fabric that concealed everything but their eyes and their bespangled and tattooed hands and feet. Paul had learned enough prior to arriving to surmise that these Arabs were either on their way to pray in one of those far-off mosques or assemble for a family meal of figs, dates, and leavened bread heated on an open oven outside the corrugated metal shed where they lived.

It was soon too dark to observe anything other than an occasional light ahead. By the time the bus arrived at the naval air station, all Paul could see was the enlisted man on duty holding a flashlight and leading him to his room. He put down his bag, undressed, and collapsed into sleep.

As soon as he awoke the following morning, he threw the covers aside and stepped to the open window where he took in the view of his new, sun-drenched surroundings. The sight of the Atlantic Ocean in the distance and the towering irises just below, along with the appealing aroma of jasmine in the air, brought him excitement and wonder. If only a half-naked nymphet would now appear at his door, one wrapped in the delicate weave of sheer tulle hanging in folds from her well-formed hips!

There was a knock in that direction. "My god!" he uttered aloud, grabbing his bathrobe and moving swiftly to open the door. There, instead, stood an enlisted man who announced, "Sir, I know you arrived late last night, but if you'd like breakfast, it's only being served for another half hour. I'm assigned to this floor. I'll have your room made up as soon as you depart for the officers' mess."

"Thank you. I'll get dressed right away," Paul stammered. He quickly put on his khaki uniform and hastened to breakfast. His role on the base was in the legal department, but he wasn't required to report for duty until the next day. He had not yet gone to law school, but prior to his flight to Morocco, he was sent to Navy Justice School for six weeks to learn how to operate as a litigator in court-martial cases. He did intend to become a lawyer after his service in the navy, but as long as he had successfully completed his six-week course, law school trained or not, the navy viewed him as qualified to perform in the courtroom.

After eating alone in the large empty mess hall, he decided to explore the base. He started down the path toward the main gate. On either side were expanses of meticulously leveled lawn, almost like carpeting. In every direction, he saw groups of Arabs on their knees, each caring for an assigned patch of green. Standing over the nearest of them was a man dressed in Western garb, presumably a local Frenchman hired to oversee them. As Paul watched, the man moved to supervise another group planting what he later learned were date palm bushes and young pomegranate trees that would one day evince a honey fragrance. The walkway he was on started upward, and when he reached the top and could see the downward slope, off to the right was a golf course and on the left, two sets of tennis courts. So far the only thing that didn't fully resemble a 1950s suburban scene back home was the Arabs tending the grass, flowers, and fruit trees.

The base encompassed acres of land. There were two airstrips near the edge of the ocean, and Paul watched as the jets and cargo planes flew in from the Sixth Fleet. He sat on one of the high bluffs that overlooked the Atlantic Ocean and gazed for more than an hour as the flights took off and landed. By noon he made his way back to the mess hall and sat himself down at a table of fellow officers. There was an O'Day, a Flaherty, a Gardner, a Hanson, and a Walsh; each of whom had that straight-laced, clean-shaven appearance of young naval officers. Paul could easily tell by their names and their looks that it was highly unlikely there was a Jew among them, but even so, he had that uncontrollable urge to wonder about it, which he always did at each new encounter.

As he sat there looking over the group at the table, Paul's earlier encounters with non-Jews raced through his mind. He had made friends with them at his prep school and had sought to be like them, attending the required religious service at the Protestant chapel each morning where the chaplain would invoke the name of Jesus Christ repeatedly as he bellowed forth about good and evil. At times during the service, the students, including Paul, had to stand erect and sing "Rock of Ages." They would also recite prayers that almost always concluded with the words "Father, Son, and Holy Ghost."

Paul's indistinguishable name further helped him blend into that world, at least until one day in his second year. A classmate approached him from behind and blurted out of the silence, "Well, at least I'm not a Jew." Paul stopped and stared as his offender mockingly swaggered off into the distance. He didn't run after him. Even though he was stunned and angered, the words and how they were uttered somehow reminded him of who he really was. From then on at chapel each morning when it came time to invoke the names of the Christian triumvirate, he refused to participate. Instead, he whispered the names of three of his guys—"Abraham, Isaac, and Jacob."

Those memories quickly lapsed as he responded to questions at the lunch table about what his course was like at Navy Justice School and his assignment on the base. None of the others there worked in the legal department, though several had served as jurors in court-martial cases. As lunch ended, Gardner mentioned that he was driving into Port Lyautey in the afternoon, so Paul arranged to hitch a ride with him. He was anxious to see during daylight the intriguing world that lay beyond the confines of the guarded and pristine naval base.

"I'd like to get to a car dealer in town," Paul said. "I gathered from the talk at lunch that most of you guys have your own cars."

"That's right. I'll drop you off at the best place," said Gardner. "I'll only be three blocks from there on the same street. The local pharmacy is a few doors from where I'm going. If you don't actually buy a car today, meet me at the pharmacy when you're ready to go back. I'll show you where it is when we get to town. If you don't arrive by five, I'll assume you drove back in your new car."

As they entered Port Lyautey, Paul saw only French faces on the streets. "Do the French and Arabs live apart?" he asked.

"Absolutely. That's true in every sizable town in Morocco. It's like the whites and colored in our country," he replied, seemingly pleased that he had drawn the analogy.

"Are there any Jews here?" Paul asked.

"I have no idea," Gardner abruptly answered. "I'll drop you off now. The dealer is right down the street. The pharmacy is a few blocks that way." He pointed in the opposite direction. "You can't miss it."

Paul made his way to the showroom. After looking over the various cars, he got the price of one he liked and thought he could afford. If his father would advance him most of the money, he could repay him from a portion of each paycheck. He told the dealer, who spoke decent English, that he would be back as soon as he could pay for the car he wanted. As he left, he decided to take a circuitous route to the pharmacy so he could get a fuller view of what Port Lyautey was like. The streets in the French Quarter were paved, as against what he would later find in the medina where the Arabs lived, and those houses he could see were of a distinctly European design. Other houses, presumably larger ones, remained hidden from view behind crenulated stone walls partly blanketed by trellises of jasmine and sprinkled all along the top of their wide heights with firmly embedded shards of cut glass, apparently to protect against unwanted intruders. Paul was struck by this kind of fortification in what otherwise seemed like a tranquil Moroccan town. What also drew his attention were the contrasting colors—the whitewashed stone walls offset by the rich blues and greens of painted doors and entryways.

The commercial street he ventured on was filled with shoppers. He stopped at a bakery to take in the display of luscious-looking patisserie. He moved next door to scan the North African wines and spices. Most of the stores seemed on the verge of closing, which he subsequently learned was a daily three-hour ritual about this time. He finally made his way to the pharmacy, and as he approached, he saw Gardner standing in front waiting for him. As they drove back to the base, Paul reported on his time in the showroom and excitedly described what he saw on the streets. Gardner listened, a bit bemused at this new arrival's reaction to a scene which he had now come to know so well. In response to Paul's questioning, Gardner told him about his role on the base, which involved using his ability to read the kind of Arabic spoken in North Africa to interpret communications that were intercepted from countries in the region. He was housed in a windowless structure where he spent much of each day studying the intercepts that were placed on his desk.

This ride back and forth from Port Lyautey was one of the few times Paul saw Gardner for more than a year. What seemed like a budding friendship failed to materialize. Gardner's work site turned out to be quite far from the legal department where Paul handled his court-martial assignments, and their sleeping quarters were in separate buildings distant from one another.

Paul was also making new friends as his first months passed. From them he learned something of the larger picture of events in the region. There was a war taking shape next door in Algeria, which would ultimately be much fiercer than the one that had now largely ended in Morocco. The two countries had different relationships with France. For the French, Algeria belonged to France in the same way that Alaska belonged to the United States. The French claimed to own it and were prepared to fight the indigenous Arabs ruthlessly to maintain that ownership. Morocco was not the same. Much of it had been under the aegis, not the ownership, of France for decades, and while many of the French who were born in Europe ventured to Morocco to live and hopefully thrive there, it was never treated with the same sense of possession as Algeria. Only months before Paul's arrival, the French had relinquished their protectorate role to the Moroccan monarchy, which proceeded to put down any civilian unrest and secure to itself all but a small portion of the country near Tangier which remained in the hands of Spain.

It was in the interest of the monarchy to keep the French inhabitants from leaving. The French model of government had been established and maintained since the early 1900s, and a smooth transition by the Arab elite meant that many of the government personnel who were French kept their jobs and only slowly trained Arabs to take their place. More importantly, the economy was largely run by the French. Except for land and businesses owned by the monarchy and its privileged entourage, most Arabs were employed in national and local French-owned companies. The breakdown was not unlike what Paul had seen on his initial walking tour of the naval base: groups of Arabs cutting grass and planting flowers and bushes overseen by a French supervisor.

Chapter 2

Paul reported for duty the next morning. He was ushered into the office of Lt. Cmdr. W. Frederick Carlson, the head of the legal department, who bluntly greeted him. Carlson had a pronounced accent, which Paul quickly sensed was a Texas twang. He spoke at a staccato pace, repeatedly making the same point as though he were herding cattle to market.

"Miner, your desk is back near the file cabinets. You will be shown there and presented with stacks of documents containing transcripts of cases that have been completed. They have to be organized and filed. Proceed to do so."

Carlson then repeated his instructions. He went on, not unlike a schoolmarm, ordering him to study a few of the transcripts after he finished his organizational work to learn what really occurred in the courtroom.

After several days of tedious reading and filing, Paul was finally told to take a few hours off and go observe a special court-martial case that was underway. He raced over to the courtroom in the next building. As he entered, he saw the judge, a lieutenant commander, and three other officers serving as the jury, seated in their respective positions. An American flag rested on a pole behind the judge on the elevated platform from which he presided. Paul took a seat in the back row. There was nothing elaborate about the courtroom—no baronial setting like Paul's image of a courtroom back home. The proceedings were being transcribed by a stenographer who, before typing a sentence, would first repeat it through a rubberized mouthpiece that reduced his voice to a whisper.

An enlisted man was on trial for violating the Code of Military Justice by sexually accosting an Arab woman. Paul gathered from the testimony that the accused had made his way south to Marrakech—how he got there was not clear—and even though dressed in civilian clothes, he stood out in the Arab souk. When he cornered and exposed himself to an unmarried young female there, one whose headscarf rested on her partially exposed shoulders, someone immediately reported him to the local police. He was arrested and turned over to U.S. military personnel in the area who ultimately sent him back to the naval base.

After the prosecutor rested his case, the accused took the stand and testified that the Arab woman had misinterpreted his approach to her. He was lost and only meant to ask her for directions. That was the only testimony the defense provided. In his closing argument, the prosecutor laid it on the accused. He told the jury that the enlisted man had been lucky. If the accosted woman had been married with her husband standing nearby, he might well have been swarmed over and beaten by a gaggle of angry Arab men. He concluded with a tone of contempt in his voice, asserting that this would have been the Arab way of rendering justice, unlike the fair trial he was fortunate to be receiving.

Paul was struck by the prosecutor's words. He wondered if members of the military on the base generally characterized Arabs that way. He thought about the Arabs he had seen on the night of his arrival as well as the ones the next day tending the grass on the base. He asked himself if it occurred to the jury that Arab justice, as it was described, was quite similar to what had once been common practice among the Puritans of New England and continued to be among many Southern whites in Mississippi, Georgia, and Alabama.

Paul carefully watched how the officer acting as defense counsel handled matters, particularly cross-examination. That was the role he hoped to play in the near future, though not in a special court-martial. In the beginning, he would be involved in summary proceedings where there was only one officer acting as both judge and jury and the offenses—gambling, drinking on duty, or stealing an item from the navy exchange store—were not serious, carrying sentences of thirty days or less in the brig. It would only be later that he hoped to qualify to serve in a special or even, one day, a general court-martial.

After another week of his day-to-day drudgery, Paul was finally assigned to act as defense counsel in his first summary court-martial case. His immediate superior in the department informed him that he would be defending Seaman John Spoor who was behind bars awaiting trial.

"He's charged with theft," the officer said to Paul. "The hearing will start in the early afternoon. Go to the brig right away and meet with him."

"The trial's going to start today?" Paul asked, sounding startled.

"That's right, Ensign. Get moving."

"Yes, sir."

Paul hastily walked down the hall to where the seaman was confined. His nerves had tightened as soon as he was told that he would actually be defending someone, but as he approached the brig, he imagined himself performing in a courtroom and felt a sense of excitement. As he gazed through the bars of the cell door, Spoor looked to him like a hapless teenager. He was sitting on the floor with his eyes trained on his crotch and didn't bother to get up to salute when the cell door opened.

Paul introduced himself and asked Spoor to relate what he remembered. Spoor just kept his eyes focused on his crotch as though he were somewhere else.

"Look, your trial starts this afternoon, and I'd like to help you. I can't if you don't tell me what happened."

Spoor finally seemed to come to. "I'm sorry, sir. I was listening to the music in my head."

"Say that again."

"I get caught up in music even when it's not on. That's why I'm in the brig. I was doing that and forgot to pay for some records at the navy exchange store. The guard there jailed me."

"I assume you're talking about phonograph records. Cowboy stuff. You sound like you're from that part of the country."

"Yeah, I'm from Oklahoma, but it wasn't cowboy stuff. It was Gilbert and Sullivan. You know, 'Yeoman of the Guard,' 'The Gondoliers,' 'HMS Pinafore.'"

Paul was floored. Here was a kid from some small town in Oklahoma who knew more about Gilbert and Sullivan than he did.

"What did you tell the guard when he stopped you?"

"I told him what I told you. He didn't believe me. He hauled me right off to the brig."

"Do you have any buddies who know how you feel about Gilbert and Sullivan?" Paul instinctively asked.

"Yeah. A bunch of us share the same Victrola. I listen to their crap, and they let me listen to my Gilbert and Sullivan operas."

"Give me the names of a few of your bunk mates and tell me where I can find at least one of them."

Paul quickly left the brig and went straight to Spoor's barracks. As he entered, the enlisted men snapped to attention. He told them who he was looking for. One of them directed him to Seaman Ralph Dillon who was sitting on the floor next to his bunk. There on the table was the Victrola. Paul ordered him to get up and questioned him about Spoor and his passion for Gilbert and Sullivan. He immediately sensed that Dillon would be a helpful witness, so he told him to pick up some of Spoor's albums and follow him to the brig.

"I can't leave before the petty officer inspects my bunk," said Dillon. "I've got to be sure the quarter bounces back up."

"What quarter are you talking about?" Paul asked with some irritation.

"The one the petty officer drops on my bunk. That's why I stay clear of it after I make it."

In spite of his impatience given the pendency of the trial, Paul was intrigued by what Dillon said. "Tell me again why I found you on the floor."

"So I don't muss up my bunk. The petty officer drops a quarter on it, just a regular quarter. If it don't bounce back up far enough for him to catch it, I got to go march in the sun for an hour. That's why I don't bother my bunk or let anyone else bother it. I stay on the floor and guard it 'til it's inspected."

Paul took a quarter out of his pocket and dropped it on the bunk from chest level. As it bounced back up, he caught it, opened his fist, and showed the quarter to Dillon. "Now, Seaman Dillon, pick up those albums and come with me. You're going to be a witness for Seaman Spoor. If it comes to that, I'll tell the petty officer that I caught the goddamn quarter as it bounced back up from your well-made bunk."

The summary court-martial proceeding began promptly at one thirty. The prosecutor sat at a desk facing the judge. Paul and Seaman Spoor were seated parallel to the prosecutor also facing the judge. There were two rows of benches behind them. The guard who arrested Spoor was sitting in the front bench as was Seaman Dillon holding Spoor's albums on his lap. The court reporter with his rubberized mask sat right next to the witness box. As the judge entered, everyone stood up.

"Be seated," the judge ordered. "If there are witnesses in the room, they should step outside, except for the accused."

The two witnesses left the room. The prosecutor made his opening statement, telling the judge it was a straightforward case of theft from the navy exchange store which his witness, the guard, would testify to. He went on to assert that Spoor was probably one of the seamen who stole goods, in this case record albums, from the exchange store and sold them to the French or Arabs in town. He concluded by stating that it was an open-and-shut case which only required him to call one witness.

Paul had decided to defer his opening statement until he put on his case, so the prosecutor proceeded to have the guard brought to the witness stand. Just as the guard entered the courtroom, Paul's superior officer from the legal department also entered and took a seat in the second row. Paul immediately knew that he was there to see how he handled himself in his first case. The guard was sworn in and during his direct testimony stated that he observed Seaman Spoor leaving the exchange store without having first gone to the cashier to pay for the albums he was carrying. He followed

Spoor on his way to the barracks, stopped him, and confiscated the albums. He then took him to the brig. The prosecutor showed the guard the albums, and he identified them as the ones Spoor was carrying. Paul did not object as the judge accepted them in evidence. That concluded the direct testimony, and now it was Paul's turn to cross-examine.

"Did you ask Seaman Spoor why he didn't pay?"

"Yes, sir. He said he just forgot. Said he was so excited to find the records he just plain forgot."

"You didn't believe him."

"No, sir."

"If you'd believed him, would you have let him pay and not taken him to the brig?"

"I guess I might have. We've had other seamen taking things from the exchange, though, and selling them in town."

"These other seamen, do they pay for what they take from the exchange?"

"Most of them do. You know, everything's real cheap at the exchange."

"How many albums was he carrying?"

"Three."

The judge asked to see the albums. He looked them over carefully and faintly smiled. Paul abruptly ended his cross-examination.

"I have no further questions, Your Honor."

The prosecutor stepped forward to conduct redirect questioning of the witness.

"Did you see Seaman Spoor leave the exchange without paying?"

Before the witness could answer, Paul rose and stated to the judge, "I object. That question has been asked and answered in his direct testimony."

"Objection sustained," asserted the judge.

The prosecutor seemed a bit frazzled. He finally said, "I have no further questions. I rest my case."

"Ensign Miner, do you have an opening statement?"

"Yes, Your Honor. Seaman Spoor has always paid for the Gilbert and Sullivan albums he previously bought and never resold any of them in town. In the instance in question, you will have to weigh his credibility about forgetting to pay. I think you will find his testimony believable. Now I would like to call my first witness."

"Proceed."

Seaman Dillon entered the room and took the stand. After testifying that Spoor listened to Gilbert and Sullivan operas whenever he could and naming the various albums he held on his lap, Paul sought to introduce them as evidence.

The prosecutor practically shouted. "I object to both his testimony and the introduction of the records as evidence. It's all irrelevant. It has nothing to do with his stealing the records he was caught with."

"Defense counsel, what is your response?" stated the judge.

"Your Honor," said Paul, "if you give me a little leeway, I'll demonstrate how this all fits in."

"Very well, but you better be able to quickly show me their relevance or I won't permit any further testimony on that, and I'll grant the prosecutor's motion to exclude the albums."

"Seaman Dillon, do you know whether Seaman Spoor's albums you brought with you were bought and paid for at the exchange?"

"I'm sure they were. Each of them has the exchange's stamp on it which says 'paid' and the date. All the dates are during the last several months."

"No further questions, Your Honor. When I call Seaman Spoor, his testimony will also show the relevance of the other albums."

The prosecutor proceeded with his cross-examination, once again stating that all the testimony of the witness was irrelevant, to the point where Paul could see the judge becoming irritable with his repetitiveness.

"Take a look at the albums that actually are in evidence and tell me if you see any exchange stamp with a marking that says 'paid'?" asked the prosecutor.

"No, I don't see any."

"No further questions, Your Honor."

"I have nothing on redirect for this witness. I'd like a brief recess before calling the accused."

"I'll give you a very short break, but that's it," said the judge. "We'll be in recess for ten minutes."

Everyone rose as the judge left the courtroom. Paul went out in the hall with Spoor and pulled him aside.

"I've been watching the judge. I think he knows something about Gilbert and Sullivan. It's only a hunch I have, but it seems to me worth pursuing. When I call you to the stand, I'll ask you questions about the incident itself, but I won't ask any about Gilbert and Sullivan. If my hunch is right, the judge will want to ask those kinds of questions. I hope you know as much as you say you do."

"I know a lot. I've listened to Gilbert and Sullivan since I was a kid."

"In case the judge doesn't want to ask any questions about Gilbert and Sullivan, I'll have to do it."

They went back into the courtroom. Spoor made his way to the witness chair and was sworn in. He testified to essentially the guard's testimony about being confronted by him.

"Do you own the albums Seaman Dillon brought to court?" Paul asked.

"Yes, sir."

"Did you buy those at the exchange and pay for them?"

"Yes, sir."

"Did you ever try to resell any of them off the base?"

"No, sir. Never."

"And would you have paid for the ones you left the exchange with if you hadn't been so excited?"

"Yes, sir. Yes, sir. I begged the guard to let me go pay, that I plain forgot, but he wouldn't listen."

"No further questions, Your Honor."

"Cross-examination," said the judge, turning to the prosecutor.

"I have only one question. Did you leave the exchange without paying for the albums in evidence?"

"Yes, sir, I did."

"No further questions."

At this point, the judge addressed the prosecutor. "As you know, I'm acting as both judge and jury here, so even if I've let counsel for the accused elicit testimony you object to, I can give it as much or as little weight as I choose depending on my view of its relevance. It won't hurt your case that I listened to it. Now, let me turn to counsel for the accused. I do have a few questions, but if you have any redirect questioning first, why don't you proceed?"

"Your Honor, I may or may not have some questions, but I'd prefer to wait until after you've asked your questions, if you don't mind."

"Okay. Mine shouldn't take long." Looking at the accused, the judge stated, "Seaman Spoor, you say you know a lot about Gilbert and Sullivan. I know a little myself. This will help me decide whether you're telling the truth. I'll start with this question: What is your favorite Gilbert and Sullivan opera?"

"'The Mikado.'"

"Do you know in what country it takes place?"

"Yes, sir. Someday I hope I get to Japan."

The judge went on. "Was 'The Slave of Duty' a Gilbert and Sullivan work?"

"Yes, sir. That's another name for 'The Pirates of Penzance.'"

"Now answer this one for me. What is the name of a Gilbert and Sullivan opera that this court-martial is not?"

Spoor thought for a moment. Then he laughed. "I know. It's 'Trial by Jury.' There's no jury in this trial—except you, of course."

"One more question. What was the name of Gilbert and Sullivan's business partner?"

The prosecutor looked relieved when the judge asked that question. Paul wondered if Spoor could possibly know the answer.

Spoor promptly replied. "It was D'Oyly Carte. D'Oyly was his middle name, but that's how he was known. I can't say I remember his real first name." He paused. "Oh, yeah, now I remember. It was Richard. He played music, but he was really the business guy who made Gilbert and Sullivan's pieces successful from a money standpoint."

"I don't think we have to go any further," the judge stated. "I accept Seaman Spoor's account that he forgot to pay. Seaman Spoor, the charge against you will be dropped and you are free to return to your barracks on the condition that you go to the exchange and pay what you owe for the albums. Then you can have them. The guard will go with you and explain to the cashier what this is all about."

"Yes, sir. Yes, Your Honor. I'll never let it happen again."

Everyone rose as the judge left the courtroom. The prosecutor limply shook Paul's hand and immediately departed. Seaman Spoor thanked Paul profusely. Paul's superior walked up and said, "Ensign Miner, what made you think the judge would ask those questions?"

"It was just a hunch I had after observing him. I knew it was risky. I was ready to explore the subject on redirect if I was wrong, but I didn't want to have to do it because the judge would think I coached him with the answers."

"Ensign Miner," he stated, "for your first case you did a hell of a job, a hell of a job. There will be more to come, more to come."

Chapter 3

Paul received praise the next day from several of his colleagues in the legal department who heard about his performance from his superior. There was no word from Lieutenant Commander Carlson, however. Paul was told that there were several upcoming summary court-martial cases to which he might be assigned as defense counsel. They all involved seamen charged with relatively petty offenses, and he was to study their cases in order to be prepared to act on their behalf.

That evening after dinner, he decided to see if he could find the Franco-American Club in town. He had only had one other occasion to venture into Port Lyautey since his first trip with Gardner and that was solely to purchase a new MG convertible that his father had recently advanced him the money for. He spoke a little French and was anxious, at long last, to meet some local people. He had heard about the club at meals in the officers' mess, including the French women who gathered there to entice American naval officers with their charms. He got into his MG and drove to that part of Port Lyautey where the club was located. It was behind one of those high stone walls, but the lighted sign outside was clear enough to assure him he had arrived at the right place. His uniform made his entry unquestioned by the guard.

It isn't as though the French in Port Lyautey weren't used to seeing Americans. It was now more than a decade since the Second World War when U.S. troops landed on Media beach some five miles from town. The naval air station, which the Vichy initially established and the Free French then gained control of, was ultimately taken over by the Americans and much expanded.

As Paul gazed around the crowded room for someone he might know, his eyes lit on Arlen O'Day who was talking to two women. He had met O'Day in the officers' mess hall that first day and seen him several times since. He walked over to them, and O'Day proceeded to introduce him to Lise Novikov and her daughter Tanya, both of whom spoke excellent English. The older woman's name didn't sound particularly French, so Paul asked her where she lived before coming to Morocco.

"I was in France, in Paris, but I am not French," she said with a warm smile. "My daughter and I are Russian."

Paul's eyes widened. She saw his reaction and went on. "Real Russians are very much the same as Americans," she said.

"Is your husband with the Soviet Consulate?" Paul asked hesitantly.

"Please tell Ensign Miner how it is you're here," interrupted O'Day.

"We love coming to meet and talk with Americans."

"No," said O'Day, "how it is you are in Morocco, and who you are?"

"We are White Russians. I am from St. Petersburg." She went on at length and with ease, telling Paul her family story just as she had O'Day and other Americans over the years whom she sensed were interested. "We were driven out by the Communists in 1917. My father was a count. He sent us to Turkey while he fought the Reds in the south of Russia. Fortunately, he was able to escape and join us after he and his fighters were defeated. We had to leave behind our possessions, our wealth, and all our former way of life. We went from Turkey to Paris and finally to Morocco. My husband's family had much the same experience. He now works as a supervisor in a French-owned farm cooperative nearby. I give private lessons in

Russian to local people and Americans from the base. It is not St. Petersburg but we live on."

What immediately came to Paul's mind were his forbearers who belonged to a persecuted people who struggled to survive in a Russia over which this woman's ancestors ruled and thrived. Yet in the face of her family's former station of nobility, he found himself drawn to her. She conveyed an openness that was most appealing, particularly to a young man who, while excited to be on his own adventure in a foreign land, had already been far from home for quite some time. She was wearing a modest paisley dress and second-hand black shoes, but for all her unadorned appearance, there remained an air of regal stature about her. In the meantime, her daughter Tanya gazed intently, even longingly, at O'Day. She had plainer features than her mother, presumably stemming from her father, and was obviously smitten with O'Day's good looks and outgoing manner.

Paul was struck by his unexpected encounter with Madame Novikov for another reason. Before arriving in Morocco, he had decided to read those novels he was exposed to in college but only casually studied. He had fortuitously started "Anna Karenina" while on the flight to Morocco and by now had finished it, having underlined words to look up and lines, paragraphs, and passages to which he was drawn. As soon as it seemed appropriate, he told Madame Novikov what he had read.

"You must be familiar with the book."

"Yes," she softly replied.

"I'm much taken with Tolstoy's writing. I haven't read any biographies of him. As I read "Anna Karenina," I found myself wondering what he was like as a person."

Madame Novikov momentarily said nothing. She was hardly the boastful type, but she liked what she saw in Paul, so she decided to tell him more.

"My parents and grandfather knew Tolstoy well. They also knew some of the people he portrayed in his novels. For all I know, members of my family are in there too."

Paul was startled. He struggled to know where to begin.

"Did Anna Karenina actually exist?"

"I never heard my parents say so, but Tolstoy knew people who moved in the same circle. Rumors always circulated about unfaithfulness in one generation after another, even passionate attachments like the one between Anna and Vronsky. I don't think Tolstoy needed much else to take it from there." Before Paul could respond or ask more questions, she stated, "I will tell you more later, but first let me hear your name again."

Paul sensed that she wanted to know about him before she talked further about herself and her past.

"It's Paul Miner," he replied.

"What kind of name is that?" she asked. "You Americans are of so many different stocks. Russians are, too, even if we all look broad-beamed and grim." She laughed, further disclosing to Paul how well she spoke English. "So where is your family from?" she went on.

"My father grew up in a small town in middle America."

"Is that mining country? Was your father a miner?"

Paul was amused but stayed silent. He just smiled. She continued.

"People in Europe often get their last names from the work of their ancestors. Of course, there are other ways of inheriting names. You'd think the Russian counts and countesses, like my family, were always aristocrats. I do trace my roots to a Russian general who fought Napoleon, but the family began as aristocrats only several hundred years before, not like, you know, the people of Moses."

Paul kept his silence. Was she playing down her own past to get him to say more about his? Did she already know he was Jewish?

Suddenly Tanya jumped in. "To be a general in the Russian army before 1917, you had to come from the aristocratic class. Our family owned much land near St. Petersburg starting in the 1500s.

My mother and father and all those before them had many servants and lived in mansions."

"Tanya, please," Madame Novikov asserted, facing Tanya with a stern look. "Let's talk about him," she said, meaning Paul. "So," she asked, "did you get your name because there was a miner in the family?"

Paul finally responded. "No, I'm not sure how we got our name. Maybe it wasn't always that name. Maybe it was changed when my father's family came to America."

"Where did his family come from?"

"My father was born in Poland."

"You know, much of Poland was once part of Russia. Maybe your father is Russian like us."

I'm sure not like you, Paul thought to himself. He could also see that she had no idea he was Jewish. "No, he isn't Russian," he finally said.

"So you're Roman Catholic. You won't disappoint me if you're not Russian Orthodox. There aren't so many of us anymore."

Paul slowly responded. "I'm not Catholic either." She looked at him curiously. Something inside him said not to put on a Protestant charade. The truth just came out. "I'm Jewish."

There wasn't the slightest pause. "How wonderful! I've never really known a Jew. We are just like you–driven from our land."

Given the pogroms in Russia under one tsar after another, to hear what appeared to Paul a genuine expression of delight from a member of that aristocratic class was jarring. The thought floated through his mind that among those Communists who led the revolt in 1917 were Jews who detested the tsar and all those who benefited from his rule.

Before Paul could say more, the lights overhead began to blink, indicating that the club was about to close for the night.

"I guess I have to go now," said Paul.

"You must come to our home to meet others in the family and talk more. You will hear from me through Arlen."

The next few days passed quietly since no new court-martial cases were yet assigned to Paul. During his free hours, his exhilaration over meeting Madame Novikov channeled itself into rereading chapters of "Anna Karenina." He imagined Madame Novikov as a younger woman but somehow could not fit her into the world of Tolstoy's Anna. Regardless of that, the images he drew from what he was reading made him eager to visit her at her home, perhaps even to meet other Russian women who might better fit the role of the beautiful and adulterous Anna.

The opportunity soon arrived. O'Day saw him at breakfast and pulled him aside. "I've been meaning to tell you how much Madame Novikov enjoyed meeting you. She's fascinated by your being Jewish. She'd like to have you come to her house tomorrow night, if you're not on duty. I'm going, so let's not drive separately. You can ride with me. After we eat, Tanya and I are going to the Franco-American Club. You can stay at her home or come with us. Whichever, I'll give you a ride back."

"I assume her husband will be there. What's his name? Are any other family members coming?"

"I'm sure Nikita will be there. He's a jovial, roly-poly fellow who speaks only a touch of English. He's hard not to like. I don't know who else is invited."

"I'll knock on your door at six."

Paul spent his free time before the next night reading about Tolstoy's Anna and Vronsky and Kitty and Levin, to the point of fully expecting to find at least one of them at Madame Novikov's. He bought a box of chocolates at the exchange store—his mother had taught him good manners—and expectantly rode into town with O'Day.

The Novikov home was not a grand villa behind a high wall, but it was built of the same whitewashed stone and as such must at least have been a small reminder for the Novikov family of those bygone days in Russia. Nikita greeted them at the door, and, indeed, his loose trousers surrounded a rather substantial belly.

"Come in, come in," he said in his heavy accent.

The women were in the kitchen preparing blini and rice kasha with mushrooms for dinner. Madame Novikov heard Nikita bring the boys into the living room and entered from the kitchen to greet them.

"Welcome, welcome. Please sit. Nikita will bring you some vodka. We never begin a meal without it."

After they settled on the living room couch and as Nikita brought in a full carafe of vodka, Madame Novikov said to Paul, "We make our own vodka."

Wishing to sound appreciative, Paul asked, "How is it made?" The only thing that came to mind was the bootleggers in the 1920s.

"It's very easy. First, we take tap water and boil it. We pour in as much alcohol as there is boiled water and continue boiling. The grocer keeps a full supply of grain alcohol for us. After a bit, we pour what's in there through a strainer to get out the impurities. It then goes into the refrigerator overnight and at some point, a flavor, like tarragon, can be added. For us, it's like drinking water. So here it is."

Nikita handed each of them a small shot glass filled from the carafe he was holding, raised his glass, and uttered some Russian phrase. Everyone took a drink, then another. The drinking continued throughout the meal. After dinner, Paul decided to stay behind while Arlen and Tanya left for the Franco-American Club. Arlen promised to be back in about an hour to give Paul a ride to the base. Madame Novikov proceeded to tell more about other Russians who had made their way to Morocco—family members, friends, and acquaintances from the prerevolutionary era. A number of Russian families lived in each of the larger Moroccan cities—Tangier, Casablanca, Rabat, Marrakech. She had family in Tangier. They would be coming for brunch this Sunday.

"You must please come," she said to Paul.

"Thank you. I certainly will if I can."

"You will enjoy them. When we are together, we have much fun, and, of course, drink vodka. Alexander, my brother-in-law, strums the Russian guitar and sings. He is very playful. It is his family that once owned much land in and around Moscow. You can't help but like him. My sister is dour, even stern, but she loves music and teaches it. Then there is my niece, Lila, who is about your age. She is married to a Frenchman who is off fighting in Algeria. She is like her father. You will see."

By the time O'Day returned for Paul, Nikita was half-asleep in his tattered armchair, sipping vodka whenever he awoke. Paul was sitting on the floor, his arms clamped around his raised knees, fascinated by the stories of Madame Novikov's Russian past.

"I know you must go now, but when you come on Sunday, I want to hear your stories," she said as Paul departed with Arlen.

Chapter 4

The next morning Paul found his way to the barbershop after breakfast. He would need a haircut before the Sunday brunch. The barber was new, a native Moroccan—his skin was olive-colored and his hair black and curly—but at least all his equipment was the same as before when a seaman was doing the cutting.

The Moroccan motioned Paul to the chair, placing the striped gown around his neck and spreading it to his knees.

"Don't give me a crew cut, just a normal haircut."

The barber nodded and added, "I understand."

Paul could see and feel that he knew his craft. After cutting his hair the way Paul wanted, he applied shaving cream to his sideburns and the back of his neck. He carefully used a straight razor to smoothly shave the creamed areas close and clean. This was the part of the haircut Paul always enjoyed the most.

"You are an excellent barber. It's nice to see that local Arabs are hired to do work on the base."

The barber smiled.

"How did you get the job?"

"My friend works on the base. He makes sure the grass and flowers are kept right," he slowly replied, searching for the best way to say it. "He told me they needed a barber."

"I think I saw your friend when I first arrived at the base. He was supervising the workers who were cutting and watering the grass. But he looked French, not Arab."

"He's not French, and he's not Arab."

"What else could he be?"

As the barber removed the gown, he slowly answered, "He's Jewish. So am I."

Paul looked flabbergasted. As soon as he overcame his reaction, he quietly asked, "Is there a Jewish community in Port Lyautey?"

As he stared at Paul's white face, officer's uniform, and American haircut, the barber hesitantly replied.

"Yes."

Paul sensed his concern. He stayed silent for a moment, and then, lowering his voice, said, "Don't worry. I'm Jewish too."

The barber's eyes widened. He put his arm on Paul's shoulder. "I am surprised. You are an officer. I didn't realize they let Jews become officers."

"Well, I wouldn't say that the U.S. Navy is brimming with Jewish officers, but there are some. Over time, you're even likely to cut other Jewish hair on the base."

"We are Sephardic Jews. We have been in Morocco a long time."

"When did your ancestors first come?" Paul eagerly asked.

"They have lived here ever since the Romans drove the Jews from Palestine or maybe even before then. They left for Spain or Portugal a thousand years ago but came back after the Catholics forced them to become Christians or be killed."

This man wasn't just a barber, Paul thought to himself. This was a knowledgeable man who made his living as a barber.

"Where do you live in Port Lyautey?"

"Almost all the Jews live in the 'mellah' near the Arabs. Our part is separate from theirs. There are some Jews living in the French Quarter. We don't see them much. I don't think they want to be part of us, part of the Sephardim."

Paul felt a stir of emotion. The barber could see his reaction. He once again put his arm on Paul's shoulder.

"I am Moshe," he said.

"I am Saul," he replied. He had not uttered that name since he was a small boy. His father had told him to always keep it a secret.

"Aside from your friend, are there other Jews working on the base?"

"Yes. We trust the Americans. If you do a good job, you keep it. We Sephardim do good work in any job we get. We always come on time. We stay late if we have to. We know that's what the Americans expect. That's our way too."

"Would you take me for a visit to the mellah?" Paul blurted out.

"Yes, for sure. But you must wear your uniform. I want my family and friends to see an American officer who is Jewish."

"Certainly," Paul said. "Do you have a day off? Perhaps I could come with you then, if I am free."

"I must work every day but Sunday. That is the day off on the base. I should go to synagogue on Saturday, but if I do, I lose my job."

"I will see you in the middle of next week. By that time I should know if I can make it the following Sunday."

As he moved to the door, Moshe walked with him. "You know," he added as Paul listened intently, "my ancestors may have been among those Jews who were exiled from Palestine after the destruction of the First Temple thousands of years ago or some of the ones who rebelled against the Romans and were driven out after the destruction of the Second Temple." He wanted to be sure Paul knew that.

They firmly shook hands, and Paul left. The unexpected discovery of a Jew in his midst, a different kind of Jew, moved him. He suddenly felt those very early years of his youth coming back, those years when he was Saul. He punched his fist into the palm of his hand as he rapidly walked to his room. He sensed an almost biblical jubilance in meeting a Jew who could trace his roots so far back.

One of the books Paul brought with him was a collection of maps of the Middle East. He immediately opened it to check the distance from Jerusalem to Morocco. It gave him an understanding of how long it took those departing Jews to cross North Africa on foot. Egypt, Libya, Tunisia, and Algeria were in between. Many of the wanderers must have settled in one or another of those countries while the rest moved further westward to Morocco.

Paul's excitement sparked him to go straight to the base library. He was hoping to find books on the Middle East and perhaps even on Israel, a subject he had paid little attention to in the past. Upon his arrival, he found that among the journals the library collected was a supply of back issues of American magazines with articles on the Middle East by distinguished writers, several of whom had

Jewish names. Paul gathered a number of the most recent ones and seated himself at a library table.

Since he was not due at the legal department until early afternoon, he had time to absorb a great deal of information and opinion over the next several hours. He learned that beginning in 1948, hundreds of thousands of Sephardic Jews spread from the Arab countries in the east to those all along the North African coastline began to depart for Israel just after its recognition by the United Nations. They left behind the land they owned and almost all of their personal possessions, which the Arabs quickly confiscated. Significant numbers of other Jews from northern and eastern Europe—Ashkenazi Jews—had arrived before Israel was formally recognized, many at the turn of the twentieth century and later in the 1930s as Hitler came to power and systematically annihilated the Jews.

One article dealt with how the Sephardim had lived in relative peace but as a distinct minority among Arabs in countries east and west of Palestine, at least until the Second World War when the Vichy French and Nazis in North Africa ghettoized many of them into concentration camps in Tunisia, Algeria, and Morocco. It revealed that there had been pogroms in that part of the world over the centuries, though not with quite the barbarity of those in Europe and Russia.

Another article focused on the life of the Sephardic Jews who migrated to Israel. Even though they had finally escaped their second-class status among the Arabs, to Paul's distress, the article talked about how, upon arriving as free citizens in Israel, they found themselves treated as socially inferior to the white-skinned Ashkenazim. The article went on to make much of how the treatment of the Sephardim in Israel was comparable to that of eastern European Jews who immigrated to America around the beginning of the twentieth century. The Jews from Germany and Austria who had landed some fifty years before looked down on them. There were some among the earlier arrivals who went out of their way to welcome and reach out to the eastern European Jews, but it took a long time for the barriers of separation to begin to break down in the United States. The article's hope was that the same thing would happen in Israel. It stressed that in some ways, just as the evil of Hitler helped bring Jews together in America, the hatred and jealousy of the Arabs before, during, and after the creation of Israel would ultimately bring the Ashkenazi and Sephardic Jews together, if not among the first generation of arrivals, then perhaps among their sons and daughters or their grandsons and granddaughters.

Chapter 5

The time for brunch on Sunday at the home of White Russians didn't start until about two in the afternoon and went on for hours of vodka. As Paul stepped into the Novikov foyer in his civilian clothes, he was greeted with kisses on both cheeks by Madame Novikov and taken by the arm into the living room. She immediately commanded him to no longer call her Madame Novikov. Henceforth, she was Toitia Lise.

As he entered, the first person he saw was Tanya sitting next to Nikita. O'Day was not at her side. Paul had not seen him for the last few days and did not seek him out. Perhaps it was a sixth sense that things were no longer the same between him and Tanya, since otherwise O'Day would have talked to him about riding together to the brunch. Perhaps it was Paul's desire to be the only American there when he came upon Lila. In any event, O'Day was not there, and Tanya was looking grimly Russian.

"This is my sister, Nadia," said Toitia Lise.

Nadia strode forward and firmly shook Paul's hand, looking domineering and solemn. Paul always enjoyed the challenge of those kinds of looks. He squeezed back just as hard and stared straight into her eyes. Then he smiled, which actually brought forth a smile from her.

"And this is my brother-in-law, Alexander. He will soon be singing for us."

Alexander put his arm on Paul's shoulder and he, too, smiled, but this was not at all forced. He was holding a guitar and strumming it intermittently. He, like Nikita, spoke very little English and was not as tall as Paul had expected, appearing quite similar in size and appearance to pictures Paul had seen of Tsar Nicholas during the First World War.

And then there was Lila. She smiled just as her father had, and the glow of that smile penetrated Paul as he had hoped it would. There was none of her mother's grimness about her, though there wasn't an abundance of warmth either. She was womanly, like his image of Anna Karenina. Her features were straight and unmarred. She seemed not to have any of the physical attributes that Paul saw in the other Russian women in the room—only those he had read about in Tolstoy's renderings. Her hair was curly blonde, her cheekbones high, her eyes almost as blue as the Moroccan sky, and her body firm but tender. For Paul, her tenderness came to the fore through his sighting of her breasts hidden yet accentuated by the simple red dress she was wearing.

Paul was sitting next to Toitia Lise. As soon as he took a sip of the vodka, its warmth ran down his insides, as had his first sighting of Lila, and he now had the courage to look directly at her. She smiled, not shyly, and joined the others in singing in Russian as her father played the guitar. Paul tried hard not to focus solely on Lila, though he feared everyone noticed his gaze. The drinking and singing continued until they all assembled at the dinner table.

"I've told you where Paul is from," Toitia Lise said in a mixture of English and Russian, addressing the others at the table, "but you should hear from him what it is like to live there. We've only read about it and seen it in the cinema. Of course, we've heard from other Americans about their country, but it would be good to know how you see it."

Given her previous reaction to his being Jewish, Paul assumed she wanted to hear how a Jew saw America.

"You know, I have had all the advantages of being born and growing up there—my family, my schooling, and now as an officer in our navy. But Jews still are largely not accepted. The private school

I went to took only a limited number of Jews, even though many who were denied entry had much better qualifications than most of the non-Jews who were accepted. In my town, Jews pretty much live in their own separate area. That's also true of other groups—the Irish, the Italians, the Poles, the Ukrainians—and, of course, the Negroes are ghettoized. At least we're not the only ones who are singled out, although there are even places in America with signs that read 'No Jews, No Negroes, No Dogs Allowed.' It's certainly better than in most parts of the world"—Paul didn't want to mention Russia before and after the tsars—"but we still have a long way to go. For all of that, though, I'm thankful to be an American."

For a moment, no one said a thing. That may not have been what Toitia Lise expected to hear from Paul. Then Lila spoke.

"I think you know about our past. We feel separated too. I suppose if I had grown up in Russia before the family was expelled, I wouldn't have known what it was like to be separate. It's not as though we're discriminated against here. But we're not French. I married a Frenchman who's off fighting the Arabs in Algeria. I wish he weren't there, and I feel sorry for the Arabs. The Russians here live in the French section of each town, and we're not treated like the Arabs, but, as I say, we're not seen as equal to the French either."

Everyone took another sip of vodka, and the conversation turned lighter. Suddenly, Alexander strummed his guitar and announced something in Russian. Toitia Lise responded. "Yes, let's go on a mushroom hunt. Paul, you will come with us. The forest is close by. It's a very Russian thing to do."

Nikita and Alexander led the way, and Paul followed with the women. It was only a short distance before they reached the tree line. Paul wanted to stay close to Lila, so as the group separated on their hunt, he headed in her direction. She was on her knees searching for a mushroom as Paul approached.

"It takes a little practice to know which are the good mushrooms. My father taught me the difference when I was very young. The good ones are usually the most difficult to find. They're often hidden under shrubs and brambles. We love the adventure."

Paul was struck by the ease with which she invoked English words like "shrubs" and "brambles." In looking down at Lila, he was even more struck by her lovely breasts, which she seemed only partially to hide.

"Tell me about your husband."

"He's an architect. His parents are very French. I don't get along with his mother. She's, how do you say it, very haughty. Fortunately, Michel is more like his father. He was drafted into the army and sent to Algeria soon after we married. I hope he will at least come back for a visit soon. I live with my parents while he's gone. And you, do you have a girlfriend? You're too young to be married."

"I'm twenty-two, not so young. No girlfriend. You look quite young too."

"Thank you, but I'm older than you. I'm twenty-three," she smilingly responded. "Oh, Toitia Lise is calling. It's time to go. Maybe you'll come to visit me at my parents' house one day."

"I will," Paul replied.

Paul thanked Toitia Lise and Nikita and said good-bye to everyone. It had begun to grow dark as he got in his car and rolled back the top. As he drove, his hair was blowing in the wind, and every few yards he briefly looked up into the sky. There was a flood of stars, but each time he only saw Lila's beautiful smile. He arrived at the base and pulled up to his quarters. He went straight to his room and descended onto the bed, firmly closing his eyes so he could better absorb his image of Lila. She was that half-naked nymphet who had finally come through his door, her well-formed hips wrapped in the delicate weave of sheer tulle, her breasts fully exposed. He was so transfixed by the sight of her that he fell asleep in his clothes.

Chapter 6

Paul called Lila within days of the mushroom hunt to arrange to visit her when he had some free time. Before seeing her, though, he wanted to explore the mellah with Moshe, whom he found alone in the barbershop.

"I'd like to come to your home this Sunday, if that would be possible."

"Yes, fine. Remember, you must wear your uniform."

"Of course."

Paul arranged to meet him Sunday morning near one of the medina gateways and walk from there to the mellah. They found each other at the appointed spot and proceeded to that part of the medina that abutted the mellah, all the time glancing at their Arab onlookers who stared at a fully uniformed naval officer in their midst.

Paul sensed an air of pride in Moshe as they walked together. The decrepit corridors of the medina were just wide enough for typical European cars to slice through. The low-flung buildings they passed were poorly constructed, and the air smelled from food being cooked on their rooftops. Paul was taken by the sight of women peeking at him through shuttered windows, of children begging for coins, of men whose feet were drenched in colorful dye.

Arriving at the mellah, Moshe pushed the wooden entry gate aside and led Paul a short distance to what appeared to be a courtyard. It was encircled by a portico which shaded many doorways, each draped with cloth to cover the opening to the living space of separate Sephardic families. In the center of the courtyard sat a heavyset man surrounded by young, attentive children.

"I assume he's their teacher. Is he speaking to them in Ladino?" Paul asked. "It doesn't sound French."

"It isn't Ladino either. It's Hebrew," Moshe replied.

"So this is a class in some part of the Torah?"

"No. They are being taught about the war between Israel and the Arabs," said Moshe.

"But why in Hebrew?"

"I will tell you another time."

They moved to the nearby synagogue built not unlike an Arab mosque. As they entered, Paul watched the worshipers in bare feet on the dirt floor reciting their prayers. Even though he was militarily dressed to the nines, none of them departed from their ritual to stare at him. They bowed and swayed individually and in unison as they marched about the room, each at his own pace and in his own direction. Here, there were only men. They were holding their prayer books, not perpendicular to their chests but straight up and down, parallel to their faces, intoning some part of scripture. Whenever one of them stopped, he would still continue his movement by rocking back and forth and up and down.

The only familiar sight for Paul was the rabbi on an elevated bema from which he read sections of the Torah. From time to time, he would step down with a small prayer book and walk around the room with his students, almost as though in a trance, continuing to recite and chant the prayers he was reading just like the others. The Torah had been left open awaiting the rabbi's return to pick up where he left off. Paul stood close against one wall so as not to interfere with any of those moving about, all seemingly in their own enraptured world.

Moshe nodded to Paul as if to say it was time to leave. What Paul observed there seemed ancient, a replay of prayers and gestures that had been performed exactly the same for thousands of years. In that sense he found it worth remembering, but only for historical and cultural reasons, not religious ones. There was nothing like that at his Reform Temple in America; it was more like what he once observed at a Catholic service with a friend in church. The various priestly rituals he had seen, while more elegant and formal than what had gone on here, were, from Paul's standpoint, similar theater.

Moshe led Paul back to the courtyard. He pulled aside the cloth drape that covered his family's entryway and invited him to step inside.

"My wife and children wanted to be here," he said, "but they had to go with her brother to the hospital to see their mother. She is old and very frail. They went to the French hospital. We don't have one in the mellah, and there isn't one in the medina either."

Moshe's home consisted of one large room, which served the living, dining, sleeping, and kitchen needs of the family. It had an Arab flavor, Paul thought, with cushions to sit on while eating at a table close to the floor. Other cushions elsewhere in the room were for conversation and sleep. There was no bathroom in sight.

"Those in the synagogue were very, how shall I say it, observant," said Paul. "They follow the rituals of Judaism in a way that most American Jews don't, at least in my world of American Jews. Many of us go to Rosh Hashanah and Yom Kippur services, and we usually celebrate Pesach. In English we call it 'Passover.'"

At that point, Moshe told Paul to come sit down with him on the cushions. He moved in that direction, taking off his jacket and hat.

"You should take off your shoes too. You'll feel better that way."

"Is that part of the Sephardic tradition?"

"If you mean, is there a religious reason for doing it, no. The Arabs do it for that reason, not us. It's just our way."

Paul sat down in the comfort of the cushions. Moshe picked up on Paul's remark about Pesach.

"We like Pesach best, too. Even though we are poor, we try to include anyone in our community who does not have family nearby. We say 'Let all who are hungry sit with us.' We use the large plate on the shelf above the kitchen sink," he said, pointing in that direction. "It has been passed down for many generations."

Paul rose and walked to the kitchen shelf. He ran his hand over the saffron-colored ceramic plate. Moshe assumed Paul knew something about what was placed on the plate, which was actually true even in the face of his family's infrequent Passover observance.

Moshe continued. "We put cilantro, lettuce, roasted egg, and lamb bone on that plate and add a spoonful of charoset. We have matzah which we hide under a pretty cloth. And we set aside a silver goblet for Elijah. The Haggadah tells us to remember that the Promised Land is within the reach of each of us. It tells us that this year we are in bondage, next year we shall be free. It tells us this year we are here, next year we shall be in Jerusalem."

Paul decided to change the subject. "I suppose most Jews live in mellahs throughout Morocco," he said.

"That's true. As you can see, the mellah is similar to the ghetto in Europe. Until not long ago, the ones here in Morocco had high walls. Nobody could enter or leave after it became dark, just like the ghettos in Spain and Italy. My grandparents lived in one like that in Fez. Some still have walls, but now it isn't as hard as it was for them. At least we can move around and work for you Americans and for the French. But we still live apart, by ourselves, even if there no longer are high walls."

At that point, Moshe excused himself and went out into the courtyard. When he came back, he said he was sorry but he had to go to the hospital to be with his wife and children. Paul quickly rose, reassembled himself in his military garb and shoes, and walked with Moshe to the mellah's gate. He thanked him as Moshe led him back through the medina to where Paul's car was parked.

That was Paul's only visit to the mellah. He would stop by the barbershop in the ensuing weeks for a haircut or just to chat, but he could not get Moshe to say why the teacher had been instructing the children in Hebrew. Moshe would only put his finger to his lips whenever Paul inquired further. He finally stopped asking.

Paul had not seen Moshe for quite some time, so he decided to drop by, but Moshe was not there. Another barber motioned him to the chair.

"I'm not here for a haircut. I came to visit Moshe. Where is he?"

The new barber haltingly responded that he had just been hired to take Moshe's place because Moshe had failed to report for work for over a week.

"He was a friend of mine," said Paul.

"Are you Ensign Miner?" the barber asked.

"Yes. How do you know my name?"

"There is an envelope here for you. It has your name on it."

The barber handed it to Paul. When he got back to his room, he sat on his bed and opened the envelope. There was a letter inside. This is how it read:

Dear Saul,

You wanted to know why the students were learning Hebrew when you visited me at my home in the mellah. I can now tell you. It is because Hebrew is the language of Israel. I am writing this to you during Pesach. Remember when I said that this year we are in bondage, next year we shall be free. This year we are here, next year we shall be in Jerusalem. It is now that time. I and my family and thousands of other Sephardim from the mellahs all over Morocco are secretly departing for the Promised Land after two thousand years of wandering in the desert. Maybe one day you will join us.

Your friend,

Moshe

Chapter 7

During the week after Paul's visit to the mellah, he set out in his MG convertible to visit Lila. The two-lane highway to Tangier was a continuation of the same one he had been on the night he first arrived at the naval base. He could see the Atlantic Ocean on his left as he raced past the sub-desert and brush. It was actually hard to separate the sea from the cloudless sky except for the infrequent site of a naval vessel.

At the same time that Paul was racing to what lay ahead, Lila sat in the garden of her parents' modest but comfortable home. She knew Paul was attracted to her, but her willingness to see him also reflected her sense of his naïveté and boyishness. As a married woman with her husband off fighting a war and her only friends a few other women, she was lonely. Even if Paul sought more of a closeness than she was prepared for, at least at present, she was sure she could handle him. Other men, Frenchmen as well as sophisticated Arabs, had certainly made advances toward her, but she easily put them off, more because she wanted males to talk to, not submit to. Still, she longed for male companionship but of a kind that was safe and with someone who was interesting and different. What could be more interesting and different, and at the same time safe, than an ingenuous American who was Jewish? Maybe he would be like the brother she never knew.

Paul arrived in Tangier around noon. Though the white stone walls and other exteriors there offset some of the sun's heat, it was still very warm at midday in the early Moroccan spring, so women thought nothing of dressing quite casually as they made their way through the streets. As he slowly drove along, he even observed some women openly breast-feeding their infants, apparently thinking nothing of it. Men who walked or drove past them, except for an occasional American like Paul, were completely unflustered by the sight.

It was nearly an hour before he was due to meet Lila. He knew he would need time to find where she lived. Prior to coming, he had talked to one of his friends, a fellow officer named Mark Milford. Mark was an intelligence analyst who spoke Russian. He had told Paul that once he arrived in Tangier, he must look for a Russian restaurant on the main thoroughfare. The restaurant's name was "Le Cosaque," which in English meant "The Cossack." He should stop there and get specific directions. The owners were his friends; he often practiced his Russian with them, and, in fact, had talked to them about Paul. They would surely know Lila's parents, the Gatusovs.

Paul soon observed the restaurant's sign and pulled over. He parked nearby and walked to the closed front door. He knocked hard, and the door soon opened. A white-haired man appeared.

"I hope you are Monsieur Lenikov," said Paul.

"Yes," he answered in English. "We're not open quite yet."

"I am Paul Miner from the American base in Port Lyautey. Mark Milford told me to come here and say hello."

"Ah, yes. Please enter. I am just making the bar ready for our clientele at noon. My wife, Sonia, is in the kitchen directing the Arab help, but she will be out in a moment. Can I get you a drink—on the house, as you say?"

"No, thank you. I need some help to find where a Russian family lives, the Gatusovs. I have the address. Perhaps you know them."

"We all know each other. We do not know the Gatusovs well—they come here only occasionally—but I know where they live. It is not far."

"Thank you."

"Mark spoke of you the last time he was here. You are his friend, the Jewish officer friend, aren't you?"

"Yes." Paul said nothing more than yes. The question was a quick reminder of what appeared utmost about him in the mind of others. Yet so far, at least among the Russians he had come to know, his Jewishness seemed to reflect their attraction to him. He was determined to assume the same of Monsieur Lenikov.

"Here is my Sonia now. Sonia, this is Paul Miner, the American officer friend of Mark that he has told us about."

"How nice to meet you!" she said. "We always enjoy seeing Mark. His Russian is excellent, and we give him good practice."

"I assume you are in a hurry, so let me tell you the directions you need. By the way, please call me Vladimir. Maybe you will come back today, even for a late lunch or dinner."

"If I can, I certainly will."

"I actually have something for you that I would like to give you before you go," said Vladimir as he walked over to a pile of documents and lifted a folded one from the top. "After we talked about you at Mark's last visit, I thought if you ever came, you would like to have this. It is a map of Judah and Israel. It is dated 1691."

Vladimir unfolded the creased map and placed it on one of the restaurant tables. It looked to be about four feet wide and three feet long, and across the bottom it had stains, ones that made it seem its age. The stains didn't cover any part of the map drawings themselves, so such sites as Jerusalem, Hebron, Tiberius, Jaffa, Gaza, and hundreds of other lesser known places were all there. On the top left corner and the lower right were huge Latin inscriptions and embellished drawings which added to its Romanesque flavor. Paul, whose eyes were nautically clear, poured over all the names, both the familiar and unfamiliar ones, and tried to figure out what the Latin words meant.

"May I know how you obtained this?" he asked as he continued to gaze at all the map's depictions.

"I collect maps. I have hundreds of them. When we lived in Paris during the War, I would search old bookstores for any that were interesting."

"I couldn't possibly afford to pay you what this must be worth."

"As I said, Mark told us about you, and from what he said, I thought this map would be of interest to you. I cannot vouch for its authenticity, so it may only be worth a modest amount. I have given others away to friends and good customers. I can see by the way you study it that it has meaning for you."

"I must give you something." Paul reached into his pocket and pulled out a $10 bill. "Please, at least take this."

"No. It is a gift. I like giving gifts."

Vladimir proceeded to tell Paul how to get to the home of Lila's parents. As Paul left, he took the $10 bill from his pocket and unobtrusively placed it under an ashtray at the bar. He had folded Vladimir's gift to him back into its creases and lightly tied it with string. He wrote Lila's name on the back of the top fold and penciled in the directions Vladimir gave him.

He found his way with relative ease. As he approached the front door, he saw Lila sitting alone in a wicker chair in the side yard. Her back was to him as he moved in her direction, and he could see her blond hair nestled to her neck and her bare upper back absorbing the sunshine.

"I'm here behind you."

"I know you are. I heard you coming through the grass." She stayed seated, looking straight ahead. He circled around her, bent forward, and extended his hand to hers, she pretending to be a countess, he her lieutenant of the guard. They both laughed.

"What a good day to be here! Your garden is lovely."

"Thank you. My father has worked very hard to make it so pleasant. I delight in just watching the flowers from my chair."

They sat for a few minutes, neither saying anything more, perhaps not knowing who should say what. Paul finally broke the silence. "Why don't we go somewhere for lunch? I hope you haven't eaten yet. Actually, I've just come from that Russian restaurant, Le Cosaque. I stopped there to get the right directions to your house. My friend Mark goes there to practice his Russian from time to time. The owners seemed quite nice. Maybe you would like to go there for lunch."

"No, I would not," Lila replied, with a sudden firmness that surprised Paul. He did not pursue the matter further, and, at Lila's suggestion, the two of them strolled down the street to a French restaurant. As they entered, the maître d' ushered them to a table by the window.

"I thought you might wear your uniform," she said as they sat down. "It makes you look a little older, dear brother."

"Next time I will wear it," he said, partly encouraged that she made a warm reference to him as her brother, partly disappointed that that's how she viewed him, even with his colorful ascot aristocratically tucked into the unbuttoned opening of his collar. "I'm practicing for when I go to Spain on leave. We have a naval base in Rota, but one of the conditions Franco imposes is that no one can wear a uniform anywhere outside the base. He doesn't want any of the Communist diplomats stationed at consulates around his country to think that he's that close to us."

"What is a 'leave'? Is that some kind of vacation?"

"Yes. That's what we call it in our navy. It's like a vacation for a week or two. You earn it by the amount of time you serve. Whether I'm on leave or not, I can easily arrange to come see you."

She laughed, and it made Paul feel good. It also furthered their sense of togetherness, to the point that after finishing lunch, they sat by the window for several hours talking more intimately about each other's lives: how and where they had been educated, what their parents were like, Paul's sense of being Jewish as an officer in the U.S. Navy, the death of Lila's brother from tuberculosis before her birth when he was only five, how Negroes were treated in America, why Lila married when she was just under twenty—on and on until Paul suddenly realized that he'd better start back to the naval base.

"We'll have lunch soon again. I'm sorry to hear about your brother. Maybe I can take some of his place."

"Yes. You can be like a brother." What was going through her mind was finding an excuse to have a male friend. She would describe him as her American brother, and even if others did not believe her, she would treat it as true.

They walked back to her house, said good-bye, and he drove off. When he came to a stop light at the edge of Tangier, he decided to pull over and place the black canvas top on his MG to protect him from the wind. Part of the canvass was stuck in the upper jamb of the trunk. He opened the trunk to loosen it and there sat the map Vladimir had given him. He had intended to tell Lila about it, but he completely forgot. He got back in the car and continued his drive to the base.

Upon arriving, he was too tired to study the map further, but as soon as he rose the next morning, he spread it out on the floor of his room. He compared the rendering of Judah and Israel to the one in the book of maps he had brought with him from America. There was a difference of 265 years, but the names of the key cities were spelled the same on both maps. Paul sat down at his desk and wrote his parents a long letter telling them about his meeting the Novikovs in Port Lyautey and his trip to Tangier to visit the Gatusov home. He mentioned only that the Gatusovs had a married daughter without saying more about her. He also described the map he was including with his letter and how he had gotten it. He wanted his parents to keep it safe for him. He finished the letter and packaged it with the map for mailing.

After Lila watched Paul drive off the day before, she returned to the family garden and sat where he had found her hours earlier. She smiled as she thought more about their long conversation at the restaurant and sensed in herself a real appeal for him, even a desire, that went beyond any role he might play as her brother. They had arranged to have lunch again the following Wednesday, which she mentioned to her parents that evening while reporting on Paul's visit earlier in the day.

During the week in between Wednesdays, Paul was fully engaged in court-martial work. He handled several of the other summary court-martial trials that had been assigned to him and continued to distinguish himself as an effective litigator. By the time his next visit to Lila was to occur, his superior had decided to elevate Paul to the special court-martial level where he would soon be receiving assignments.

Lila was again waiting for him in the family garden when he arrived. Given his excitement about receiving the gift of the map of Judah and Israel from Vladimir, he repeated his suggestion that they go to Le Cosaque for lunch. Lila once more emphatically said no, and they proceeded back to the restaurant where they had been the week before. As the maître d' seated them at the same table by the window, Paul decided to question Lila further about Le Cosaque.

"Please tell me why you won't go to the Russian restaurant. Is the food not good? Don't you like the owners? Do they have a son who you were once in love with?" Paul asked with a questioning gesture.

"Let me have a sip of wine. It will make it easier for me talk about it."

After a few sips, she stated, "My parents told me several years ago that we must never go there again. You see, the Lenikovs dealt with the Nazis during the War."

This was the last thing Paul expected to hear. "They dealt with the Nazis? Vladimir Lenikov was the same man who gave me a seventeenth-century map of Judah and Israel, and he knew I was Jewish. I meant to tell you about the map. That's part of why I kept suggesting we go there for lunch. I felt a certain obligation. I've already sent it to my parents back home. Please tell me more," Paul pleaded.

"Well, I obviously only know what my parents have said. There was a whole Russian colony in Paris during the War. Since they weren't Communists or Jews, the Nazis pretty much left them alone. My parents, just like most of the other Russians, struggled to get by, but they certainly didn't do business with the Nazis—except for the Lenikovs.

"They had a large collection of valuable silverware—knives, forks, spoons, platters, goblets—everything they could bring with them from Russia or get through merchants who did business with them at their Paris restaurant. They lured Nazi officers to the restaurant by giving some of these items to them. It might have been sets of utensils one time and a silver platter another—anything to make sure their Nazi customers, their best customers, would come back.

They kept it secret from others in the Russian community. The Nazis were certainly seen eating there, but it was only later during the occupation that it became known that they were being given valuable pieces of silverware. Someone from the French underground was told about it and what I have just said was later confirmed. After the War, the Lenikovs were confronted and admitted it. They told my father and others they did it to survive. They ultimately had to leave Paris. They came here and opened their restaurant. We wanted to forgive them, to understand, so we went a few times, but we just didn't feel right about it. You hardly ever see a Russian customer there."

Paul was stunned by what she told him. His first impulse was to write his parents telling them what he had learned and to send the map back. He would confront Monsieur Lenikov with it at the restaurant—he refused to think of him any longer as Vladimir. He would slam the map down on a table in disgust and condemn him for what he had done during the War. But as he thought more about it, he knew he wanted to keep the map or at least keep it until he could determine whether it was authentic. Maybe it once belonged to a Jewish family in Germany or France. Maybe there would be some evidence of where it came from after it was examined by an expert. Maybe, just maybe, it was a small act of contrition by the Lenikovs.

"Now I understand why you don't want to go there." He let his anger die down and then turned to what he really cared about. "If I'm free next week, can we have lunch again—sister?"

"You know I will make myself free to see you—brother."

That evening, as was usual, Lila had dinner at home with her parents. About midway through the meal, she again brought Paul into the conversation.

"We've been meaning to talk to you about that," said her mother. "You must be careful to be with him very infrequently, if at all. I know it has only been on a few occasions, but already I have heard of it from others."

"Mama, I've told you about my time with him. He is pleasant to be with, and he's not like the other men I meet. As I've said, he's like a younger brother."

Alexander said nothing.

"I probably would have mentioned it even if no one else had spoken about it. But your mother-in-law has brought it to my attention. I told her it was only an innocent friendship. I think you should tell her that yourself."

"You know I can't stand her. She's going to see anything I do in a bad light."

"I agree with your mother," interjected Alexander. "You should confront her, my dear. That's the best way to handle it. Otherwise, she'll just assume the worst and then even embellish on that. And you shouldn't just tell her over the phone. You should do it in person. I also agree with your mother that you should not see your American friend when it's just the two of you. If he's invited to a family gathering at Toitia Lise's and we're there too, that's fine, but having lunch with him or just being seen alone with him only makes people talk."

Lila responded in frustration. "There is nothing like what you think between us, and I won't have our friendship destroyed through rumor." She looked down for a few moments while thinking it over, gained control, and slowly stated, "I will go to see my mother-in-law."

"Fine," said her mother. "That's a good start."

Over the next few days, Lila stewed about what her parents had said to her but finally got up the courage to call her mother-in-law and ask if she could pay her a visit.

The deCouvier mansion was hidden from view behind one of those crenulated stone walls that protected its inhabitants from intrusion. It was late morning as Lila approached. A servant ushered her through a marbled hallway to a living room decorated so ornately that one might have thought it was an impending visit to a member of eighteenth-century royalty. Lila had certainly been there on quite a number of occasions during Michel's courtship of her, so she was aware of its grandeur. Indeed, it brought to mind the stories her father had told her as a child of what life had been like prior to the revolution.

Her mother-in-law sat smartly and well-coiffed in a straight back chair near the fireplace. Lila approached and, as Madame deCouvier remained seated, she greeted her in the French fashion by pressing her cheeks, but not her lips, to both sides of her mother-in-law's cheeks.

"Please be seated," she said to Lila, pointing to a similar chair on the other side of the fireplace. "What have you heard from Michel?"

"I had a letter recently. He seems fine. He wrote that he had hoped to come home for a visit next month, but due to the worsening conditions there, that has been ruled out. I am terribly disappointed. Have you received any mail lately?"

"I have. He said much the same thing to me and his father—your father-in-law. It has been nearly a year since we have seen him."

"It is the same for me, of course."

Before Lila could say why she was really there, her mother-in-law preempted her. "I am glad you are here. I have a subject I wish to speak to you about. My husband served in the First War against Germany. He was away for nearly two years. I stayed with my parents during that whole period at our family home outside of

Paris. I never had any association with other men except my father and friends of my parents. Do you understand what I am saying?"

"I do, but surely you know we live in a different time now."

"It may be a different time, but essential values do not change."

"If you mean having an intimate relationship of any sort with other men, certainly that value has not changed. But, of course, I have had no such association." Lila retained her poise and answered without emotion.

"You have been seen with other men, one in particular and most recently," Madame deCouvier firmly stated.

"The other men are merely acquaintances. I dismiss any overtures they might make to me, just as you would, I'm sure." Lila then discreetly continued. "I do have one man who has become a friend. He is actually like a brother, a brother I never really had. He is younger than I am, and he is only a brotherly friend."

"I assume you are referring to the American officer I have heard about."

"He is an American officer."

"Others, friends of mine, are talking about your association with him. You've been seen having long lunches with him."

"Yes," Lila answered in a matter-of-fact way.

"For the sake of my son, it should cease."

"But it is only a friendship. It is nothing more." Lila thought to herself that if it ever became more, her mother-in-law could thank herself for helping it to happen.

"Whatever it is, it must stop. It is an embarrassment. I do not wish to have to inform my husband."

"There is nothing to inform him about." Lila could feel her Russian blood rising, but she stayed silent. She looked straight at Madame deCouvier.

"Have you no more to say?" Madame deCouvier asserted.

"I've said all there is to say. I wish you believed me."

"How can I believe you? You flaunt your being with this American." Her voice rose, and she looked away momentarily.

"I think I should leave," said Lila.

"Yes, leave. Leave and go to that American. Leave and go to that Jew!"

Chapter 8

Paul was sitting at his desk in the legal department. He had just finished acting as defense counsel in his first special court-martial case. Unfortunately, the seaman he defended was found guilty. The tension of preparing and making his closing argument before the three jurors, particularly in light of the guilty verdict, had left his head throbbing. His superior walked up to his desk.

"Miner, you look a little dejected. The case is over."

"Sir, I'm thinking about what I might have done differently and better."

"Suit yourself. You did as well as could be expected given the seriousness of that seaman's actions. The presiding judge told me afterward that your questioning and closing argument were excellent. But that's not what brings me here. Even though you've only handled one special court-martial as the accused's counsel, everything I see makes me think that you are quite capable of acting as a prosecutor at that level, and not long from now, you'll be ready to represent either side in a general court-martial. It helps that you'll soon be elevated to the rank of lieutenant junior grade. There are only a few officers Lieutenant Commander Carlson trusts with such an assignment and certainly none at your coming rank."

Paul was obviously pleased with the vote of confidence even though his head continued to throb. After his superior left, he quickly walked to his MG and drove straight to a deserted area of Media beach. He took off his shoes and socks and sank into the sand on his back, eyes skyward, listening to the waves, somehow expecting the Americans who had landed there in 1942 to come ashore again. He lay there until the pressure finally eased.

On his drive back, he decided to stop at the phone exchange on the base to call Lila. She probably wouldn't understand the struggle he had been through in the courtroom, but like the sky and the waves, he knew hearing her voice would soothe him. When she answered, he made up some excuse for why he called and asked when he could see her again.

"I've just had a rough time with my parents and my mother-in-law. They don't want me to see you alone or at all. They think it's not right for a married woman. I told them you were only like a brother to me." Lila mentioned her visit to her mother-in-law but said nothing about her mother-in-law's final assertion.

Paul was not sure how to respond. He hoped her reference to him as merely a brother was only her way of trying to put off her family's demands.

"Do you want to see me again or not?" he said in a firm voice.

There was a long pause. Paul just waited.

"I do want to see you. I mean that."

"Good," he asserted. "Let's figure out a way."

"Well, I actually have thought about it," she said after another long pause. "I have a friend in Rabat. My parents know her. I could arrange to visit her for a few days. I would take the train from here, and instead of going straight through to Rabat, I would get off in Port Lyautey and we could be together. You could even drive me to Rabat from there."

"That's a hell of an idea," Paul declared. "You work it out with your friend. I'll call you next week so you can let me know when you'll be coming. I'll have to make sure I can get the time off."

After the phone call ended, Paul hurried back to the legal department and absorbed himself in his work. When he called Lila back the following week, her mother answered the phone. He immediately hung up. He went to lunch at the officers' mess and afterward returned to the phone exchange and placed the call again. This time Lila answered.

"We'll have to figure out a way of reaching each other that somehow avoids one of your parents answering the phone," Paul said.

"I know. My mother suspected it might be you. I just shrugged. We can talk about it when I see you. I'm coming on Tuesday. The train arrives in Port Lyautey around eleven in the morning."

"Great. Unless I call you, I'll be waiting for you at the station."

"I've got to hang up now. My mother may come in from the garden at any moment. I'll see you Tuesday, my dear brother."

When Tuesday arrived, Paul was at the train station waiting for Lila as she stepped onto the platform. She looked quite lovely in her purple dress, her blond hair streaming down the sides of her face, her head protected from the sun by a wide-brimmed straw hat as though she were on her way to the beach. They lightly embraced.

"Hop in the car. I'll drive slowly so we don't get to Rabat too soon. It's wonderful that I get to see you again."

Once they were out of Port Lyautey, the road was largely empty with few cars moving in either direction. Lila filled Paul in on her ensuing conversations with her parents. She told him that she had tried to soothe their concern but they remained adamant about only seeing him at a family gathering. She also told him that she would not be taking the train back to Tangier. Her father had business in Rabat in a few days and had arranged to drive her back with him.

They had just passed a small village when suddenly the car's motor began to sputter. As Paul eased over to the side of the road, it completely died. He got out and raised the hood, but nothing there caught his attention. He got back in the driver's seat and hopelessly tried the ignition again.

"The various connections and spark plugs seem fine," he said. "We must be out of gas. I thought we had plenty. Even the gauge reads half-full. Maybe I can get a ride to that village we just went through and get some gas. I've got a canister in the trunk. You should come with me if I can get someone to stop for us. I don't want you here all alone."

Lila nodded. Unfortunately, there were no vehicles in sight. The afternoon sun made standing there increasingly uncomfortable. After about twenty minutes, a car did come into view heading in the opposite direction. Paul waved, and it slowed down but did not stop. He frowned at the two Arab-looking men inside as they drove on.

After a few minutes, they saw the car that had just passed coming back. It pulled up and the two men got out. They had a determined look on both their faces as the one on the driver's side slammed the car door shut. They began walking toward Paul and Lila but stopped as one whispered to the other. Paul was not in uniform and looked like a European tourist who might have a wad of money in his pocket. He drew Lila closer to his side and bent down to pick up a large stone. The two men came a few steps closer. Paul shouted for them to stop. They turned and moved toward his car. He shouted at them again. They paid no attention as they looked under the hood and started talking to each other, this time in very loud voices. They could have been speaking the Moroccan dialect of Arabic, but Lila told Paul they weren't speaking any form of Arabic she'd ever heard. There were Berbers from the Atlas Mountains in the general area who spoke their own dialect, but Lila was certain it wasn't that language either.

All at once, Paul sensed what he was hearing. The same guttural tone and nuance had been repeated time and again when he visited his grandparents. The language was rarely spoken by his parents, so he couldn't interpret the words. But he knew the sound. He knew the intonation. He stepped toward them and said in his halting French, "Je suis Juif," hoping they would understand him, but if they did speak any French, Paul's pronunciation escaped them. All they seemed to see were his blue eyes and blond hair. Suddenly, like the immediate untangling of a deciphered code, it dawned on Paul what he should do.

Slowly but firmly, he began to recite a prayer that almost every Jew has been taught, regardless of how little trained in Hebrew or whether from as far away as Argentina, South Dakota, or China. It was the prayer that reflects the Jewish concept of monotheism devised thousands of years ago. There was a chant in his voice as he practically sung the words: "Shema, Yisraeil: Adonai Eloheinu, Adonai Echad!"

The two men's eyes widened. It seemed to make no difference that Paul was still gripping the large stone in his hand and heading close to them. He had enunciated a prayer in Hebrew that tore down every barrier between them. They moved toward him with outstretched arms and embraced him. Without hesitation, without forethought, he embraced them back. Lila looked on in astonishment.

"These are Jews," Paul said to her with ostensible pride. "Speak to them in French. They will understand your words much better than mine."

Lila proceeded. Their names were Joses and Simon. She asked them whether they could share some gasoline. They understood her but said they would first like to try the ignition. Joses got behind the wheel. After trying several times, he spoke to Simon in Hebrew and told Lila in French that he didn't think the problem was a lack of gasoline. He got down on his back and crawled under the front of the car while Simon studied the engine from above. When he crawled back out, they conferred again. He went to his car and came back with a kit of tools.

Simon told Lila that there was some kind of blockage in the line that prevented all but a trickle of gas from getting to the engine. When he had tried the ignition, it sputtered and died in a way that meant the problem was not an empty tank. Paul and Lila watched as Joses crawled back underneath with several of his tools in hand and a roll of thick black tape. They heard him knocking away, and in about ten minutes he edged out on his back. After lying there for a bit, he slowly rose and motioned to Simon to get into the driver's seat. Simon eased into the seat and turned on the ignition. The engine roared back to life.

"Hooray!" Paul yelled as loud as he could. He went over to Joses and Simon and embraced them again. He turned to Lila and said, "Can you ask what prompted them to come back after they first drove away."

Lila was more than curious herself. After asking them, Joses quickly replied. He said that when they first drove by, they were already late for a family meal, but even so, they began to worry about what they had seen. They assumed that another car would ultimately stop, but they saw no cars coming in the opposite direction. Finally, Joses told Simon they must go back, at least to see if someone else had stopped to help. They turned around, and as they approached, they saw the two of them in the scorching sun.

Lila translated for Paul what Joses said next: "We knew we had to help. That is what we learn from our Judaism. We didn't know you were Jewish, but God must have known and made us come back. You see, we fix cars in our town. That is our work. God knew."

Lila turned to Paul. "How wonderful! We should give them something."

Paul knew they wouldn't take any money. He was right. As soon as Lila reached into her pocket and held forth some francs, they raised their hands as their way of shunning them. They once again stepped forward, and this time embraced both Paul and Lila. That was all the satisfaction they seemed to need.

"We will be leaving Morocco sometime soon," Joses said as Lila translated. "Simon and I will be going to Israel where we belong. After we are settled, I will take the road to Damascus to find some relatives of mine there and bring them back. I may have to sneak across the Syrian border."

Joses and Simon stayed a moment longer to make sure the engine turned over again and started for their car. The hour was nearly noon. As Paul watched, the powerful glare of sunlight from their car's front window caught him in the eyes. He felt unsteady and suddenly collapsed to the ground. Lila quickly bent down and lifted his head onto her crouched thigh. Joses came running over with a canister of water and poured it on Paul's mouth. Slowly, as he began coming to, he muttered, "I am Saul. I am Saul."

At that point, Joses, in an effort to help him back to consciousness, told Lila to ask him where he was from.

"Cilicia," he groggily answered. "I am a Pharisee."

Lila translated for Joses, and they both looked puzzled. "Ask him where I am going after arriving in Israel."

"Damascus. I am going with him."

Lila translated again, and they continued to look puzzled. At that point, Paul began coming to. He sat up, and Lila wiped his brow. "I don't know what hit me. I saw this blinding light and suddenly felt overwhelmed. It must have been a seizure. I haven't had one since I was a teenager. I feel better now."

After assuring Joses and Simon that he was all right, they got in their car and drove off. Even though he was able to keep his balance as he walked in a small circle, Paul was still a bit weak.

"Are you sure you feel strong enough to drive?" she asked him.

"Yes, for certain," he said uncertainly.

"I don't think I'd ever heard any Hebrew before. Thank heavens you were able to say those words to them! You and I have talked about what it's like being Jewish in the world you live in. Now I have seen Joses and Simon. Before the three of you, I never really had contact with a Jew. In fact, I'm sure I've told you that all I ever heard about Jews was that they were bad, that they killed Christ, that I should stay away from them."

"Yes, much of the world sees us that way. Certainly there are Jews who are not good people, but most of us try to do the right thing. Have you ever heard of Mark Twain?"

"Yes, the great American writer."

"I have an essay of his in my room. I want you to see it. He wasn't a Jew, so his words are those of an outside observer. His essay was written more than fifty years ago, but it could have been written yesterday. It's called 'Concerning the Jews.' He was born just before our Civil War, and during the early years, he had very unpleasant thoughts about Jews. But that changed over time, and his essay is about how he came to see the Jews in a different light. It paints us as pretty damn special. I think it might mean something to you. I will give it to you the next time we're together."

As they moved toward the MG, Lila, while walking by his side, put her arms around Paul's waste and placed her head under his arm. They said nothing, but a warmth and closeness radiated from each of them. They got in the car and slowly proceeded to Rabat, gripping each other's free hand for long periods but still not speaking. When they arrived at the friend's house, Lila said in a gentle tone, "Maybe it would be best if you didn't come in. I told my friend you were bringing me, but if you meet her, she may say something to my father when he comes to pick me up. I'm sorry. Let's talk over the telephone after I get back to Tangier. We will somehow work out a way to see each other soon again."

Paul drove off. He arrived back at the base and spent that evening reading Mark Twain's essay. The next morning he went to the legal department and reviewed the various documents that had collected on his desk. Toward the end of the day, his superior casually dropped by and hinted that Lieutenant Commander Carlson was considering his possible role as defense counsel in a general court-martial. If it happened, this would be Paul's first involvement in a case at the highest court-martial level. His superior said it was not a certainty, but Paul should be ready if the assignment arises. "I'll make sure you don't get any other cases," he went on, "until he decides on the one I'm talking about. In the meantime, finish off all the work you presently have. Either I or Commander Carlson will let you know early next week."

On the following Monday, Paul decided to call Lila. She would have returned to Tangier by then. He was dwelling on what his superior told him and wondered when he might be able to see her if the big case came through. He at least wanted her to know that he might be tied up for quite some time. He also wanted to hear her voice. He placed the call, and again Lila's mother answered. This time Paul did not hang up.

"Is Lila there?"

"Is this Lieutenant Miner?"

"Yes, it is, Madame Gatusov."

"Lila is not here now." She said no more.

"May I ask when she might be back?"

"I cannot say." There was a trembling in her voice.

"Has something happened to her?" Paul pleaded.

"Lila is all right."

"Are you sure? You're not just saying that."

"No, she is okay, at least physically."

"Then where is she?" Paul kept asking.

"She's at the home of her parents-in-law."

"I see."

Another long pause.

"It's her husband," Madame Gatusov finally said.

"Michel?"

"Yes."

"Has he returned for a visit?"

"No," she quietly replied.

"Oh."

"He's been killed," she said in desperation.

"Oh my god!"

"Arab insurgents trapped him and his men somewhere in the south of Algeria and slaughtered them all. It is horrible."

"I am so sorry. I know how hard this must be for her and for you." He wasn't sure what more to say. Finally, before she hung up, he added, "You have my deep regrets. Please tell that to Lila too."

"Thank you." She sighed.

Chapter 9

Paul slowly walked the short distance from the phone exchange to the legal department, pondering as best he could what effect Michel's death would have on him. Before its impact fully registered, he was summoned to Lieutenant Commander Carlson's office.

"Lieutenant (j.g.) Miner, I know you're aware that you might be involved as defense counsel in a substantial matter. I am not yet assigning it to you. You'll understand why after I lay out the facts."

Carlson proceeded to describe the situation: An officer—Carlson did not immediately disclose his identity—was accused of an attempted homosexual assault against a prominent Arab man who had been visiting the base on official business. The Arab had lodged a complaint with the base commander. He alleged that the officer, whom the Arab knew, approached him while he was standing alone in a secluded area of the base. After greeting each other, the Arab charged that the officer, thinking there was no one else in sight, assaulted him sexually. In fact, stated the Arab, a fellow Arab who had come to the base with him, observed what happened from a hidden spot. The accused officer had asked for Paul to represent him in his general court-martial case.

"Who is it?"

"Lieutenant Gardner, Robert Gardner."

"He wants me to represent him? There are certainly more senior officers in the department who would have much greater experience."

"He requested you. I said I'd consider it."

"Even if he asked for me, why would you want to honor that request when you know it would be my first general court-martial? A homosexual attack within the confines of the base is a very serious charge, especially when it involves an officer accused by a prominent Arab."

"Look, every case you've handled, whether you've won or lost, has been handled extremely well. You're a very quick study."

"But, again, why did Gardner pick me?"

"He obviously asked around about who would be best to represent him. I talked to him too."

"Does the base commander have to take the general court-martial route? If the evidence is sufficient against Gardner, why not quietly arrange his departure from the navy. Give him a less-than-honorable discharge."

"Miner," said Carlson, "this matter is larger than Gardner alone. We are in the process of negotiating a new lease on the base now that the Arabs have taken over from the French. And this Arab gentleman who was accosted is the chief negotiator for the monarchy in connection with our future here. If we don't handle this case in a straightforward and serious manner, it may play into the hands of those who don't want us."

"Does that mean the cards are stacked against Gardner?"

"I will do everything I can to make sure things are handled according to the Code of Military Justice," pronounced Carlson.

"Permit me to think it over. I'll sleep on it and get back to you first thing tomorrow morning."

Paul left Carlson's office and went to his desk. He leaned back in his chair and put his hands over his eyes. He still remembered Gardner's stiff reaction on that ride into town when he had asked him if there were any Jews in Port Lyautey. Paul had dwelled on that response for some time but then completely put it out of his mind until now. Did Paul's being Jewish have anything to do with Gardner choosing him? Was Gardner hiding anything?

That evening, he went to a restaurant in Port Lyautey so he could be by himself and think over what was happening in his life. Even though he had been asked toundertake the most significant legal challenge in his soon-to-end naval career, the impact of Michel's death was oremost on his mind. If he took this case, he would be completely absorbed in it for an extended period, perhaps right up to the end of his service in Morocco. While he very much wanted to comfort Lila in her grief, he new her family would deem it highly inappropriate for him to attend Michel's funeral or otherwise be seen in Lila's presence. If he decided to absent himself from work tomorrow and drive to Tangier, regardless of how her family might view it, it might end up creating more distress for her than comfort.

After further mulling it over, he decided to write her a letter. He could convey his understanding of what she was going through in words, tell her that he had been assigned a large court-martial case that would keep him deeply engaged for some time, and urge her to write or call him when she felt up to it. What also played on his thoughts was the fact that he was not about to turn down the defense of Lt. Robert Gardner.

Paul returned to his room and wrote out the letter to Lila. He then stretched out on his bed and began thinking more about

Gardner. The issue of homosexuality, particularly in the military, was a terribly uneasy and unforgiving matter. The accusation alone, apart from being proven, would evoke unspoken but real prejudices among the potential decision-makers. That would be an extra burden for Paul to overcome if he were to be Gardner's defense counsel. As he lay there, he began to think about his only experience involving a homosexual. He remembered every detail as though it had happened the day before.

It was during the summer between his first and second years in college. He was hitchhiking from the south of France, hoping to make his way to Paris by nightfall. His early morning departure from Nice was under clear skies, but by noon he had only made his way to the outskirts of Saint-Vallier. He had been alone in seeking rides to this point, but he soon observed another hitchhiker ahead of him on the road. They stared at each other and instinctively edged closer. The other hitchhiker was a Frenchman about Paul's age, and the two of them soon began talking to each other in English. His name was Jacques, and he was also heading for Paris. They quickly agreed that it made more sense to seek a ride together than compete apart. It was apparent that Jacques was an experienced hitchhiker, so Paul stood behind him as Jacques thrust his thumb northward, smiling slightly at the oncoming cars.

A four-door Citroen soon pulled over, and the driver waved them in. He introduced himself as Pierre and said he was going as far north as Dijon and then heading eastward. He spoke almost no English, so he and Jacques conversed in the front seat while Paul hunched over in back trying to keep warm. After driving for several hours, they arrived in Dijon where it was raining quite hard. They proceeded to a youth hostel which Pierre knew about, and fortunately it had one room left. Even though there were just two beds, a big double and a narrow straw mat on the floor, they took it.

Pierre had brought with him some bread, cheese, and wine which he happily offered to share with Jacques and Paul in the room. Jacques took him up on the offer, but Paul, in spite of the heavy rain, was determined to have an ample meal prepared by a chef who knew how to cook good French food, even if it meant getting soaked. Pierre offered to drive him to a restaurant he knew of nearby. He also said he'd pick him up afterward at a given time. Paul had seen the restaurant when they approached the hostel and told Pierre not to bother. He thanked him and set out in the rain. After an excellent dinner, he made his way back to the room. To his surprise and relief, he found Pierre and Jacques ensconced in the double bed. The straw mat had been left for him.

The next morning, Jacques and Paul were standing together at the bathroom sink. Paul asked Jacques how he slept.

"Okay," he replied.

"What did you find out about Pierre while I was having dinner?"

"He's an experienced architect. We talked about that as we ate. I'm studying architecture, and he gave me a lot of good advice on how to proceed."

"That's nice to hear. He seems like a fine man. It was kind of you both to leave the mat for me. How did Pierre sleep?"

Jacques smiled. "He tried to get me," he said nonchalantly.

"Get you? You mean he tried to rob you?"

"No. Get me."

Paul slowly but finally understood what he meant. "You mean he's a homosexual?"

"Yes."

"What did you do?" Paul asked with astonishment and alarm.

"I told him to lay off. Then I rolled over and went back to sleep. So did he."

"Good God! I would have leapt out of bed and still be running barefoot in the rain."

"Ah, my American friend, you must develop a little savoir faire."

Jacques said nothing more about the incident, though he and Paul decided to cease their hitchhiking, pool their resources, and take the train from Dijon to Paris. After breakfast, at which Pierre spoke at length about the competing approaches to architecture in Europe and America, he offered to drive them to the railroad station.

The train ride took several hours, so the two of them had plenty of time to talk, but Jacques never brought up the subject of Pierre. For Paul's part, he decided not to raise it unless Jacques did. But as he gazed at the countryside for long periods, Pierre was very much in his thoughts. He seemed just like the two of them. He wasn't that strange or odd creature that people talked about whenever the subject of homosexuality came up. He was kind and thoughtful. After wanting to share his food, he offered to drive Paul to the restaurant so he wouldn't get drenched and said he'd pick him up. He was apparently a knowledgeable and accomplished architect from whom Jacques—and Paul—might learn much.

All this went through Paul's head as he considered whether to represent Gardner or not.

Chapter 10

The next morning Paul told Carlson he was agreeable to taking the case, subject to his first meeting with Gardner to resolve an issue that concerned him.

"Fine," said Carlson. "I'll permit that. I'll get in touch with him and have him come here promptly."

Paul immediately looked up the rules with respect to a general court-martial. He turned to the provisions involving pretrial procedure under which a section entitled "Investigation" appeared. It basically said that in the absence of a waiver, no allegation could be referred to a general court-martial for trial until a thorough and impartial investigation took place. The investigation was to involve an inquiry into the truth of all aspects of the allegations. Its outcome would be based on a finding by a presiding judge after a full hearing. The accused could be represented by counsel at the hearing and cross-examination of all witnesses was permitted. If the allegations were determined to be sufficiently truthful, the judge would recommend that the matter proceed to a general court-martial; if not, the allegations would be dismissed and the proceedings ended.

When Gardner arrived at the legal department, he proceeded directly to Carlson's office. After about ten minutes, they emerged together and walked to Paul's desk.

"Lieutenant (j.g.) Miner, why don't you take Lieutenant Gardner to the conference room? I've told him that I've made you generally aware of his situation."

The two of them immediately went there and sat down across the table from each other. "I understand from Lieutenant Commander Carlson that you want me to represent you," Paul said. "How is it you decided on me?"

"I really didn't know where to turn. I went to Lieutenant Commander Carlson because he's head of the legal department. He recommended you to me. I asked some of the other lawyers about you, and they said good things."

It suddenly occurred to Paul that Carlson had suggested him to Gardner because he didn't want a more experienced officer in that role. Carlson was doing all he could to control the outcome and please the base commander. Paul clenched his fist. He had a serious reservation about defending Gardner, though it was not his alleged homosexuality, but this maneuver behind his back only strengthened his resolve to take it on. He quickly decided not to let Carlson's plan deter him, but he still needed to explore what bothered him.

"I appreciate your selecting me to defend you, but I do have a few questions which will help me decide whether to honor your request."

"Go right ahead."

"What was your name before it was changed to Gardner?"

Gardner looked perplexed, but Paul saw him grip the armrests of his chair. "What are you talking about?"

"You heard my question. What was your name before it was changed to Gardner?"

"What does that have to do with your representing me?"

"In my eyes, everything."

"I still don't get it."

"If I'm to defend you, I have to have truthful answers from you. So I want a truthful answer. What was your name before it was changed to Gardner?"

Gardner looked at Paul, still stunned. "It's always been Gardner for Chrissake!"

Paul had controlled his composure to this point. He knew if he showed any sign of uncertainty, Gardner could escape answering the question and might well decide that Paul wasn't the right person to defend him. And Carlson's maneuver now made Paul want the case all the more. As it was, given that Gardner was a full lieutenant with seniority over him, Paul was already making a demand on him which might be seen as beyond the scope of his authority. And what if he were wrong? What if his sixth sense about Gardner's true origins was mistaken?

"I'm going to ask you one more time," Paul firmly continued, notwithstanding his inner concern. "If I don't get a truthful answer, I'm not going to represent you. Now, what was your name before it was changed to Gardner?"

Gardner sat silently for a long time with his head arched back, looking upward. Paul just stared at him. Finally, he focused his eyes in Paul's direction but not straight at him and spoke awkwardly.

"Okay, my name was changed sometime long ago."

For the first time, Paul stumbled. "Please repeat that, I mean, repeat that," he said, as though he couldn't believe what he heard.

"It wasn't always Gardner. I frankly don't know what it used to be. My parents would never tell me. And that's the truth."

"I assume whatever it was, it was a Jewish name."

Gardner said nothing. Paul kept his eyes on him. Gardner would look away and then look back to check Paul's determined expression.

At last, he replied. "Yes, your assumption is correct."

At this point, Paul softened his gaze. "I understand how hard this may be for you, particularly in light of the trouble you're in."

Gardner leaned forward and folded his hands on the table. "I will tell you more, but you must agree to keep everything I say to yourself," he stated in a way that actually sounded like a sense of relief at disclosing a long-hidden secret.

"You have my word. Besides, from the moment we sat down together, everything said by you, even if I decided not to represent you, is and will be protected by the attorney–client privilege."

"I'd like to get down to the charges against me, but about what I know on the question you asked," said Gardner, still not wanting to say directly that he came from a Jewish family, "I grew up along the East Coast in one of those exclusive suburbs. It's called Kenilworth. No Jews allowed."

Paul said nothing.

"I went to a private school which also had no Jews. I doubt if that's changed. We belong to the Episcopal Church in town, and I attended religious school there. I'm an only child, so my parents didn't have to worry that a brother or sister would tell anyone that we came from different stock than our neighbors."

"That's quite an Anglo–Saxon way of putting it," interrupted Paul.

Gardner went on without responding to Paul's remark. "My father is a lawyer, a real good one, in a firm that just has Christian partners. My mother is a housewife. My grandparents on my father's side live in Washington DC. They never come to visit us in Kenilworth. We go there, though I've only been a few times. They have their own house on a street where all the houses look pretty much the same. I only know them by their first names, Herman and Gertrude. I assumed their last name was Gardner, at least until my father said it wasn't. He wouldn't tell me what it was, and I knew not to ask. I don't know whether it was then or some other time that I found out we were Jewish, but I remember seeing things at their house that I hadn't seen anywhere else."

"Like what?" asked Paul.

"A silver candleholder. It was like the trunk of a tree with branches coming from each side."

"You mean a menorah, don't you?"

"Yes, a menorah," Gardner said almost sheepishly, as though he knew the name but was reluctant to say it. He went on. "At some point, maybe when I was a teenager and after one of those visits, my father told me we were Jewish but that no one was to know. If they found out, we wouldn't be able to live where we lived or belong to our country club and I would lose my friends. He said my mother was also Jewish. Her parents were from Hungary but left there before the War and went to England. They're no longer alive. My mother came here in the early 1930s and stayed. She has a sister who's married and lives in London, but I've never met her or any of her family. My mother and her sister write to each other. I've seen letters on a table in my parents' bedroom."

As Gardner was haltingly talking about his past, Paul was sensitive to what he was saying. After all, Paul's father had essentially changed Paul's first name to his middle name so his Jewish identity would not be quite as apparent. If anyone asked what the initial "S" was short for, he was to tell them that it was just an initial, nothing more. And his last name, which at some point was surely anglicized, could have been anyone's last name.

"You don't have to tell me anything more, unless, of course, you want to."

"Maybe we can talk about this another time. You understand that my mind is elsewhere now. I am curious, though, about what made you think I was Jewish."

"It was just an instinct I had. I felt you were hiding something. We all hide things, I know, but you were a little too Waspish, too much like a cheerleader. When you drove me into town, you were quick to change the subject about whether there were Jews there. And remember, when I was introduced to you at the officers' mess, I had just arrived. I was in another land thousands of miles from home. I was probably looking for someone who was Jewish."

By telling him he also had his fears, it helped Gardner feel more relaxed and, Paul hoped, as straight as he could be in revealing what led to the predicament he was in. He decided not to raise the question of Gardner's possible homosexuality at this point, hoping and expecting that Gardner would bring it to the fore on his own.

Paul continued. "I want you to tell me what happened. Unless you give a full and honest account, I can't represent you effectively, even if what you say is incriminating. Again, it all stays in this room. But I've got to know the real story so I can think through the best way to help you. That's one of the reasons I persisted in asking you who you really are. You've got to trust me."

Gardner proceeded to talk about what took place.

Paul would constantly have him restate this or that alleged fact and question the veracity of what he was saying until he answered in the kind of detail and accuracy that Paul was demanding. He took extensive notes as Gardner spoke, studied them, and then queried him further to explain a given statement. Gardner repeatedly asked Paul whether the notes he was taking would be kept secret, and Paul repeatedly assured him they would.

When the session ended, Gardner left and went back to his room. He was not incarcerated in the brig but had been relieved of his duties and, unless specifically instructed otherwise, confined to a restricted area until a final determination of the case against him. Paul walked directly to Carlson's office.

"You had quite a long meeting."

"Yes, sir, but it was helpful. I am willing to act as his defense counsel, but I will need time to prepare."

"Well, at this point, the trial date and time for preparation will be decided by the presiding judge. The base commander is in the process of appointing the judge and jury, and as soon as he does that, you can appear in court and seek the time period you think you'll need. I will transmit your name to the commander as defense counsel."

"If I may, sir, I think it is premature to make such appointments. As I read the rules, there has to first be a hearing as part of the investigation leading to the charge against Gardner. The judge for that is the one who should be appointed now. The hearing could result in a finding that a general court-martial is not appropriate."

"Miner," Carlson asserted, "the investigative hearing is pro forma. It's usually quite perfunctory. In my memory, none has ever resulted in the dismissal of all the allegations. It may cause a slight change or correction in the language, but that's it."

"Well, sir, based on what Gardner told me, I plan to use every legal vehicle at my disposal, and the investigative hearing is clearly one of them."

"But the allegations wouldn't have been brought in the first place if there hadn't been some investigation."

"Was there a hearing as part of the investigation? Was Gardner at the hearing? Was there any cross-examination about what he's accused of? As far as I know, none of that occurred."

"Are you saying you'll raise this issue if we go straight to a general court-martial? After all, every protection you mentioned—cross-examination, presence of the accused throughout the hearing, argument before the judge—is just the same at the general court-martial, even more so. And to be quite frank, the trial will demonstrate to the Arab monarchy that the accused is being brought to justice."

"That's what concerns me. You use the phrase 'brought to justice.' I don't want a show trial. To begin with, if Gardner is innocent and that's the ultimate finding at a general court-martial, his reputation will still be sullied and his military career either ended or deeply damaged if he has to go through the ordeal of such an open trial. A representative of the monarchy can as easily sit and observe an investigative hearing as he can a court-martial. The Arab who brought the charge is certainly going to be a witness. He may wish to have this matter heard in the privacy of an investigative hearing. For all I know, it may cause him to drop the allegations."

"I misspoke about bringing Gardner to justice. I'm sure he'll get a fair trial, particularly if you're defending him."

"I appreciate your confidence in me, sir. I still want a full investigative hearing to take place. The rules require it."

Carlson rubbed his jaw and sat silent for a few moments. "Miner," he said with a certain air of apology, "I'm afraid Gardner has waived his right to such a hearing, and he did it in writing. It was during a meeting last week at the base commander's office when he was presented with the charge against him."

"Gardner told me he had been summoned there," Paul responded, "but he didn't say anything about signing a waiver. He said the base commander advised him in your presence that he would be facing a general court-martial and had the right to a lawyer of his choice. You told him if he didn't find a lawyer to his liking, you would appoint one for him."

"That's right, but when he was handed the charge, he was also given several other documents which he was asked to read and sign—and he did. One of them was the investigative hearing waiver."

Paul leered at Carlson. "Sir, you know as well as I that signing such a waiver without a lawyer there representing his interests and in a moment of severe distress is unfair. The waiver should be revoked. I want to tell this to the base commander."

"I can't permit that. What I will do is discuss the issue with him. I'm scheduled to be at his office later today. I'll convey your position and get back to you."

At that point, Paul indignantly marched out. He sat at his desk and dwelled on what Carlson said to him. After his anger subsided and in an effort to busy himself, he pulled out the notes he took during his meeting with Gardner and organized them on his legal pad. He then left but decided not to seek out Gardner until he heard back from Carlson. After lunch, he returned to the legal department and again studied the relevant provisions of the Code of Military Justice. Around mid-afternoon, he was summoned to Carlson's office.

"I'm sorry, but the waiver stands. The base commander is adamant on the subject. He's already appointed Cmdr. Albert Getters as the judge in the general court-martial and is in the process of selecting jurors. Lt. Cmdr. James Wright is the prosecutor. You've now been formally appointed defense counsel. If it's any concession from your standpoint, the base commander has already arranged with the Moroccan authorities to halt negotiations on the future of the base until after Gardner's court-martial is concluded. He doesn't want this matter to cloud those negotiations."

"I would like a hearing before Commander Getters as soon as possible. I will raise the waiver issue with him, sir."

"I'll inform Judge Getters of your wish," Carlson snapped.

Paul now sought out Gardner and informed him of what had transpired. Gardner admitted to having signed a set of documents, including the waiver, but, as Paul suspected, he was so unnerved by the charge against him that he signed whatever was put before him. It was only after he executed them that he was informed of his right to be represented by counsel.

Chapter 11

Albert J. Getters was a tall, handsome man in his late forties who was both a lawyer and a flight commander. He had acted as a judge numerous times over the years but also spent a good part of his naval career directing younger pilots on their missions in the Mediterranean. He was told by Carlson that Paul wanted to raise the issue of the waiver at a hearing before him. Getters quickly instructed both counsel to appear in a courtroom where he had a court reporter present.

"Gentlemen, I understand there is a preliminary issue to be resolved. I have been made aware of the matter by Lieutenant Commander Carlson and am prepared to hear argument on the issue. Lieutenant Commander Wright, are you in a position to argue the waiver question?"

"I am, sir. Lieutenant Commander Carlson informed me that defense counsel wanted a hearing before you. I am ready to proceed."

"Good. I'm leaving tomorrow for several weeks. I'll be at our base in Rota instructing pilots. I will want to rule on this either right after your arguments or by the end of the day. The trial will begin around three weeks from now, assuming I don't rule in Lieutenant (j.g.) Miner's favor today."

Paul proceeded to make his case. He pointed to the language of the Code which referred to a full and impartial investigation as a precondition to a general court-martial; he also emphasized Gardner's state of mind when he signed the waiver. He reiterated the other arguments he made to Carlson, including the stigma Gardner would face from an open trial even if he were found not guilty. Wright used the points that Carlson had made to Paul about the protections which Gardner would have at a general court-martial. He also asserted that Gardner had been told to read the waiver language before he signed it. At the conclusion of the arguments, Getters looked at the notes he had taken and stated that he had reached a decision.

"The waiver was signed after having been presented to Lieutenant Gardner for reading. The accused is an experienced officer. He could have asked for more time to study its language or just refused to sign it, but he did neither. The motion to lift the waiver is denied." He continued, "The prosecutor has made a request that the aggrieved party be permitted to attend all sessions of the court-martial proceedings. Given the sensitivity of our relations with our Moroccan landlord, as it pertains to this case, I hereby grant that request. As to all other witnesses, they will be excluded from court sessions unless actually testifying, as will any non-witness observers except for a representative of the Moroccan monarchy who, I understand, the base commander has agreed may attend.

"I am obviously cognizant of the effects of a general court-martial on the accused party. Accordingly, if the jury's verdict is not guilty, upon the request of defense counsel, the entire record of the proceedings will remain under permanent seal pursuant to my order. As I have ruled, the trial will essentially be held *in camera* in order to insure the effectiveness of this ruling. If there is no further business, we are adjourned and will reconvene upon my return. In the meantime, counsel can pursue what trial preparation is permitted by the rules."

After Commander Getters rose and departed, Paul and Wright briefly conferred before going their separate ways. Wright, as the prosecutor, was not required to disclose any information or documents to assist in the defense's preparation for trial. His only requirement was to provide Paul with the identity of the person who brought the charge and permit the accused and his counsel no more than a fifteen-minute meeting with the accuser and the prosecutor. Gardner had told Paul the name of the Arab man whom he thought had made the complaint against him, but since the indictment only referred to that person as the "aggrieved party," Paul sought to confirm Gardner's assumption by asking Wright to provide him with the man's name straightaway. Wright hesitated momentarily, looked at his own set of documents and proceeded to give Paul the name. It was Hassan Fassi.

"That's all I'm going to tell you. And if you want the brief meeting you're permitted to have with Fassi before the trial, you will have to do it through me." Wright then left.

Paul walked to Gardner's room where he was awaiting word of the hearing. He reported on what transpired and gave him the name Wright had provided. Gardner confirmed that Fassi was the person whom he suspected of leveling the charge. He expanded on his association with him, which he had first alluded to in the earlier part of the week.

In the days that followed, Paul met with Gardner several times to talk about the questions that further evolved through his analysis of the facts as he understood them. He also sought information about the judge. From all he could gather, Albert Getters was held in high regard as a man who was tough but fair-minded and would conduct a trial without regard to whomever its course or outcome pleased. Nevertheless, Getters assuredly wanted to advance his career in the navy. He might conceivably succumb to the wishes of the base commander by leaning in favor of the prosecution on close rulings. While it was obviously up to Paul to present as strong a case as possible, he had to bear in mind which factual and emotional avenues would demonstrate the weaknesses of the prosecution's approach and best appeal to the judge's reputation for fairness. It was the jurors, of course, who would render the ultimate verdict, but the judge's handling of the issues and legal questions during the trial would have an unspoken influence on their view of the case as it developed.

Paul spent much of each ensuing day studying written opinions and case law that were relevant to the factual and legal issues that could arise. He also talked to potential witnesses on and off the base who might be helpful. He would meet with Gardner in the evening to calm him emotionally and reassure him that he was working hard on his behalf.

It had now been several weeks since he wrote that letter to Lila. He had heard nothing from her, and even though he left it that she should write or call him, he was unable to wait any longer. In the midst of his work, he rose from his desk and walked to the telephone exchange. He was nervous about making the call but finally got up the courage to place it. Lila answered.

"It's your brother. Is this my sister?"

"Oh, I am so glad to hear your voice. I have been thinking of you a great deal."

"How are things going for you?"

"It's been very hard, of course. People have been so nice, and I have tried to stay quite busy. The shock and despair are wearing off some. I always knew this could happen, but after a while, I put it out of my mind and just wouldn't think it could happen. And I had you."

"It's easy for me to say that I know how hard it must be for you. But I'm not experiencing what you are going through, so I can say I understand when I really can't feel what you must feel."

"I appreciate what you are saying. How is your big case?"

"I'm working very hard on it. It's quite difficult. As we say, the odds are stacked against the officer I'm defending. But I've devised a plan. I still have some people to interview. I will soon have a brief meeting with the Arab man who brought the charge. It'll be a chance for me to take a hard look at him. Enough about that. I do want to see you, but I know it is not appropriate yet."

"We can talk on the phone from time to time. It means so much to me to hear your voice. I should go now. Call me again soon. You are very dear to me."

With that, Lila hung up. Paul marched back to the legal department, feeling greatly relieved and upbeat. Upon his return, he immediately focused on arranging the interview with Fassi. He met with Wright and set the meeting for the coming Wednesday in Rabat where Fassi lived. Gardner was entitled to be present, and since Wright would be there, too, he might well instruct Fassi not to answer any of Paul's questions. Fassi could volunteer information, of course, and Paul hoped, either through his own questioning or through the presence of Gardner, to induce him to do so.

Paul and Gardner arrived in Rabat in the early afternoon. The Fassi interview was scheduled for 2:00 p.m. at the U.S. embassy. When they entered the embassy lobby, the guard had them write their names in a reception book and told them to proceed to a room on the second floor. They found their way there, and as they walked in, they saw Wright and Fassi seated on one side of a long table. Paul's request to have a court reporter present was turned down, so there would be no written record of what might be said. There would only be Paul's notes.

The setting was stark and cavernous. The room was paneled in cedar wood with only a picture of President Eisenhower on the wall. There were two chairs for them on the opposite side of the table, which was too wide for anyone to shake hands across, and the only gesture of greeting was a slight bowing of the head by "the aggrieved party" after he briefly rose. Fassi appeared taller than Paul's image of an Arab. He had a black mustache, and his skin was light brown and smooth. He was somewhere in his late thirties or early forties and dressed in an Oxford-like suit with a white shirt that was buttoned to the collar. He was not wearing a tie.

"Monsieur Fassi," Paul said, "I'm obviously speaking English, but if you don't understand anything I say, please don't hesitate to say so."

"I speak English quite well," Fassi stated with an air of assurance. "If I need any help, I will tell you."

Paul could already see that this would not be an easy witness to unstitch at the trial.

"Before I ask you any questions, let me state why we are here and what we understand the situation to be." Paul did not want the interview to start and end before he had more of a chance to observe what the witness might be like on the stand at the actual court-martial. He proceeded to set forth a synopsis of the charge and told Fassi the interview was an opportunity for him to expand on it so it was fully understood.

"Would you care to tell us more of what took place the day you claim Lieutenant Gardner accosted you?"

Fassi sat silently, his lips tight. He looked straight ahead at the wall, facing no one on the other side of the table and seemingly aloof and distant from what Paul had been saying. After a period of awkwardness, Paul repeated his question, which was more in the form of a statement. Suddenly, Fassi leaned forward.

"You have asked me a very general question. Please be more specific," he said.

Paul was struck by the language Fassi had used. It was obvious that he had been coached by Wright to say what he said. He quickly conjectured that this might be the way the prosecutor hoped to learn what kind of questions were in store for Fassi at the court-martial. Fassi would give a brief answer to whatever the next question was, or no answer at all, inducing Paul to keep asking a variety of questions.

But Paul stayed on course. "I can't be more specific unless you give me a fuller picture of what transpired."

At that point, the prosecutor whispered into Fassi's ear. They both rose.

"The interview is over," said Wright. "You have received all the information you're entitled to."

With that, they walked out of the room.

"Well, what do you think?" asked Paul after the two of them were alone.

"As you can see, he's a sophisticated Arab. He was dressed in a suit from England or France. He probably got it in Gibraltar. I have seen a number of Arabs in Port Lyautey who have crossed from Tangier to Gibraltar where they can buy well-made European clothing at very reasonable prices. His English is quite good, which is unusual given that French is his second language. Basically, I didn't see anything about him that I didn't already know. At least you got a good look at him."

"I have to find out more from people here in Rabat who know him or at least know of him. Does the communication center maintain information about key people in the Moroccan government and the private sector?" asked Paul.

"I'm pretty sure we do. I have a contact there who is sympathetic to my situation. I'll put you in touch with him. If there is such information, he would know where to find it."

The two of them returned to the base, and the following day Paul got in touch with the contact Gardner had referred to. They met and Paul was given a file containing the names of everyone in positions of importance in the Moroccan government and the business community. As Paul studied the file, his eyes focused on one of the names—Eleazor ben Arendt. Next to this name was a brief description of his business involvement, his influence in the government, and the fact that he was a prominent member of the Jewish community. Based on that, Paul called the embassy in Rabat, and through an official, a meeting was arranged with Ben Arendt at his residence in the French sector. In response to Paul's inquiry, the official assured Paul that ben Arendt spoke English.

Several days later, Paul found his way to ben Arendt's home which stood behind one of those high stone walls that he was now accustomed to seeing in Port Lyautey. When he arrived at the entryway, he pushed a buzzer. A servant appeared and opened the gate. As the two of them approached the front door, Paul observed a multicolored ceramic mezuzah on the door's right jamb. He was greeted by a head-scarfed Arab woman who led him into a grand room with tapestry on the walls and a menorah in the middle of a large round table. Ben Arendt was seated at the table, and as Paul was ushered into the room, he rose and bowed slightly. His skin was an olive color, and he had a full head of white hair. Paul stepped to where he was standing, extended his handed, and said shalom.

Until that moment, ben Arendt had no idea that Paul might be Jewish. Even with the greeting, he seemed unconvinced, assuming instead that he was being visited by a U.S. naval officer who was investigating some matter which the embassy official had only spoken about generally when he arranged the meeting. He also assumed that this naval officer had sought advice from others on the correct Hebrew word to use in this situation. He gestured for Paul to be seated, and at that point the Arab woman brought in a plate of cookies and a selection of teas.

Ben Arendt sat silent, just looking at Paul, who surmised that he was still dwelling on how this American naval officer could actually be Jewish. He decided that before focusing on what he needed from him, he first better convince ben Arendt that the two of them sprang from the same biblical root.

"I know that most of our people in Morocco have now left, but before their departure, I visited the Jewish community in the mellah in Port Lyautey."

Ben Arendt still said nothing. Paul labored on.

"President Roosevelt was thought to be a friend of the Jews, but he didn't interfere with Britain's 1939 decision to end Jewish immigration into what was then called Palestine. That decision sealed off European Jewry's last chance to escape the Nazis. President Truman did overrule our State Department and recognized Israel as soon as it was created as a nation. He had a Jewish business partner before he entered politics. But Truman placed an arms embargo on Israel in 1948 when it was fighting for its existence. And President Eisenhower has been harder on Israel. He's denied it any sale of weapons."

Paul had obviously retained much of the information about Israel that he acquired from his readings at the base library, and he put it in a light that he hoped would persuade ben Arendt that he was to be trusted. Still there was no response.

"I know that the vast majority of American Jews are just like you and the other Moroccan Jews who have not left for Israel. We love our country just as you love yours."

That seemed to do the trick.

"Forgive my English. I do understand everything you say, but I speak with some difficulty. My family goes back a long way in Morocco," ben Arendt stated slowly and quietly. "That is certainly true of many of those who left, but most of them did not know Arabs in the monarchy as I do. I tried very hard to persuade the leadership of the Jewish community to stay, but I failed. There are still about five thousand of us here, many quite old. If things change, I suppose we will leave too. But I think the monarchy needs a number of us who remain. We have influence. We are knowledgeable in finance and governmental matters. So how can I be helpful?"

Paul leaned forward in his chair and proceeded to explain the Gardner situation. He hoped ben Arendt knew Fassi and what role he played in the king's inner circle.

"I only know him casually, but I do have an Arab friend who I'm sure knows a good deal about him. I have no idea why Fassi would want to bring such a charge against your Lieutenant Gardner, unless, of course, the charge is true. I will contact my friend and urge him to see you."

Ben Arendt rose and walked over to his phone. After speaking in Arabic to someone on the other end, he put the phone back in its cradle and returned to the table. He wrote out a name and address.

"He," he said, pointing to the name he had written down, "will see you now. He speaks better English than I do. You will not have to go through any effort to prove who you are. Just state your name. He knows much about Fassi."

The home of Nabih Mouad was also behind one of those high stone walls. It was located deep within the hidden confines of Rabat's medina, and but for ben Arendt having instructed his Arab woman attendant to travel with Paul to lead him through the narrow alleyways to Mouad's address, he would presumably have never found it. She remained in the car as Paul entered the house. For the next hour, after explaining the Gardner situation to Mouad, the two of them engaged in ongoing conversation as Paul asked questions and Mouad responded. Paul understood the risks he was taking in relying on information about Fassi from a man he essentially knew nothing about, but he had no other avenues at this point. After concluding their discussion and expressing his appreciation, Paul drove the Arab woman to ben Arendt's house, once again thanked him for his help, and drove back to the base.

Chapter 12

When Commander Getters returned from Spain, he summoned both attorneys. The court-martial was to begin the following week. The jury had been selected, and Getters disclosed their names. He instructed counsel not to have contact with the jurors before or during the trial. Paul had never met any of them and in a subsequent conversation with Gardner, it turned out he hadn't either. It was a certainty, though, that the accusation that Gardner had a homosexual encounter with Fassi would not sit well with any of them. The judge also reminded counsel that the base commander had authorized a representative of the Moroccan monarchy to observe the proceedings. The observer, whose name was Hadj Radwan, was designated by the king himself and would report on the trial's progress and outcome directly to "His Highness."

As the court-martial commenced, Paul and Gardner, along with a seaman who had been instructed to assist Paul on ministerial matters, were seated at the defense table. The prosecutor sat with his legal assistant and Fassi at an adjoining table. Monsieur Radwan was in a comfortable chair facing the witness stand. As the judge entered, everyone rose. The jurors were ushered in and took their assigned places in a section perpendicular to the judge's platform. The proceedings were being transcribed by a court reporter.

"Lieutenant Commander Welch," said the judge, "do you have an opening statement?"

"I do, Your Honor."

At that point, the prosecutor walked toward the jury section, faced the jurors, and began. "This case involves a heinous crime, particularly for a U.S. naval officer. On the morning of July 12, Hassan Fassi arrived here from Rabat with a fellow member of the Moroccan monarchy, Samir Badeem, who will testify in these proceedings. They were both engaged in discussions with our base commander and members of his staff with respect to the future status of the naval air station. Monsieur Fassi will testify that during a halt in the discussion, he and Monsieur Badeem, upon returning from a brief trip into Port Lyautey, took a walk to relax and converse in private before going to the command center where the discussions were taking place. Monsieur Badeem stopped at some point during their walk and took a seat on a bench while Monsieur Fassi strolled on by himself. As he neared the top of a bluff overlooking the airfield and facing the ocean, Lieutenant Gardner appeared. Unbeknown to Lieutenant Gardner, Monsieur Badeem had gotten up from the bench and moved to a spot below the bluff and within sight of what took place. Monsieur Fassi had previously met Lieutenant Gardner at the Franco-American Club in Port Lyautey and therefore greeted him with pleasantries. At that point, Lieutenant Gardner came close to Monsieur Fassi and sought to perform a homosexual act with him. Monsieur Fassi forcefully pushed him away and raced down the bluff. He saw Monsieur Badeem at the bottom, who told him he had seen what happened. They hurried back to the command center and immediately reported the assault to the base commander. The discussions were halted while the base commander conferred with Lieutenant Commander Carlson and then summoned Lieutenant Gardner to his office. This incident is not only a serious violation of Article 7 of the Code of Military Justice, it is a stain on our relations with the Moroccan monarchy, particularly at a time when the future of this base is at stake. Thank you."

At this point, the prosecutor took his seat. "Lieutenant (j.g.) Miner, do you wish to make a statement to the jurors?" asked the judge.

"I will reserve my statement until we put on our case. I only now say to the jurors not to make any judgment until you have heard all the evidence."

"That's for me to say," Judge Getters declared sternly.

"I apologize, Your Honor."

The judge instructed the prosecutor to call his first witness. Samir Badeem was thereupon summoned from the outside lobby to the witness stand. After being sworn in, Badeem sat down. He was a slight man, thin and wiry, and dressed in a suit and tie. His English was quite understandable, though there was a nervousness in his voice as he stated his name and address. He went on to testify that he was a member of the monarchy staff and had worked with Fassi on a number of assignments prior to the current one.

"On the date in question, were you present at the naval base with Monsieur Fassi?"

"Yes, sir."

"What was the purpose of your being on the base?"

"We were discussing with your commander and members of his staff whether there should be a continuation of an American naval base at this location. We had raised certain issues in that regard, and after several hours of discussion, Monsieur Fassi and I decided it was time to confer separately. We told the base commander that it would be best if the two of us went into Port Lyautey to attend to our prayers at the main mosque, and we would reconvene upon our return in the early afternoon. When we came back, we took a walk in order to finish talking about our negotiations. We proceeded together for a while, but Monsieur Fassi went on by himself while I rested."

"Were you still able to see him?"

"Oh yes."

"What happened next?"

"I got up from the bench and moved to the bottom of the bluff. Monsieur Fassi had gone up to the top. As I watched, Lieutenant Gardner approached Monsieur Fassi. He came along the top from a different direction. He couldn't see me at the bottom because some high bushes and other growth there covered all but my face. At that point, he grabbed Monsieur Fassi by the hand, pulled him close, and embraced him. I was horrified at the sight, and fortunately Monsieur Fassi broke free and raced down in my direction. When he saw me, he said Lieutenant Gardner had tried to touch him in his private parts. We hurried back to the base commander's headquarters, and Monsieur Fassi reported the situation as I stood there. I confirmed what he told the base commander."

"I have no further questions of this witness."

"Cross-examination?"

"Yes, Your Honor."

Paul stepped forward and stared straight into the eyes of the witness, who stared back momentarily and then looked away.

"Monsieur Badeem, did you go to the top of the bluff at any point while Monsieur Fassi was standing there?"

"No."

"How far were you when you observed Lieutenant Gardner approach Monsieur Fassi?"

"I was near enough to see what was happening."

"If I told you there were two sets of footprints leading up to the top of the bluff at the time of the incident in question, yours and Monsieur Fassi's, what would you say to that?"

"Perhaps the other set was Lieutenant Gardner's."

"You testified that he approached from a different direction, so they couldn't have been his."

"How could you know there were two sets of foot prints? You weren't there."

"But Lieutenant Gardner was."

"He is lying. It is in his interest to lie."

"Suppose I told you that Lieutenant Gardner took pictures that showed two sets of foot prints leading up to the bluff."

The witness peered at Fassi, desperately seeking guidance and appearing to unspool. The prosecutor rose in his defense.

"I object," Wright asserted. "If there were any pictures taken, counsel should introduce them as evidence. We are entitled to examine them."

"Counsel, the prosecutor is correct. Please seek to introduce these pictures as evidence."

"Your Honor, I merely said to the witness, 'Suppose I told you that Lieutenant Gardner took pictures . . .' I didn't say he actually did. I wanted to see the witness's reaction, and I did."

"That is a deceptive form of questioning, particularly of a witness who is not familiar with court-martial practices."

The judge said nothing for a moment. He turned to the prosecutor. "Your objection is overruled. Presumably you had ample time to prepare this witness for his appearance here. As counsel stated, he said 'suppose,' placing the question in a hypothetical context. The jurors can make their own judgment as to his response."

"I have no further questions."

Paul took his seat. The prosecutor rose and stepped toward the witness.

"I have one question on redirect."

"Proceed," ordered the judge.

"Monsieur Badeem, I meant to have you identify Lieutenant Gardner. Do you see him here in the courtroom? If so, please point to him."

The witness raised his right hand and pointed directly at Gardner. At that point, the prosecutor concluded his examination and Paul rose.

"I do have some further questions in light of Monsieur Badeem's answer." Turning to the witness after getting the judge's approval to proceed, Paul asked, "Monsieur Badeem, you state that you were not standing next to Monsieur Fassi when you testified that Lieutenant Gardner approached. How can you be so sure it was Lieutenant Gardner?"

"I could see him clearly. As I said, I was not that far away."

"What was he wearing?"

"He was in his uniform."

"Was he wearing anything on his head?"

The witness hesitated. He once again looked searchingly at Fassi.

"I don't really remember."

"Had you ever seen Lieutenant Gardner before the date in question?"

"I object," said Wright. "That's beyond the scope of my redirect."

"Objection sustained."

"I have no further questions, Your Honor. I may wish to call Monsieur Badeem as a hostile witness when our case is presented, so I would appreciate it if you would instruct him to make himself available in the lobby at that time."

The judge responded. "I think the best way to handle that is for you to alert the prosecutor well enough in advance of the time you anticipate calling him. Once informed, Lieutenant Commander Wright is instructed to make Monsieur Badeem available to testify."

Fassi was then called to the stand and essentially testified to what the prosecutor had said in his opening statement. Paul then proceeded with his cross-examination.

"Monsieur Fassi, when did you first meet Lieutenant Gardner?"

"I think it was at the Franco-American Club in Port Lyautey. I had brief conversations with him there several times."

"Are you sure it was at the Franco-American Club?" asked Paul.

"Quite sure."

"Was Monsieur Badeem with you on any of the occasions you had conversations with Lieutenant Gardner?"

"He probably was. That's how he was sure it was Lieutenant Gardner who accosted me."

"Do you ever go elsewhere in Port Lyautey?"

"Perhaps I have been to one or two stores there and also one of the local mosques. I live in Rabat, so I have no reason to spend much time in Port Lyautey. I do enjoy going to the Franco-American Club there. I like to practice my English and meet Americans."

"Were there any military installations around the bluff when you said Lieutenant Gardner approached you?"

"I didn't see any, but there must be some. It is a military base."

"But all you saw were sand and bluffs, isn't that true?"

"Yes."

"You testified that you were taking a walk with Monsieur Badeem. What was it that drew you to that part of the base?"

"Nothing in particular. It was a nice spot to look out onto the ocean."

"I have completed my cross-examination," said Paul.

The base commander and Lieutenant Commander Carlson were called to the stand. The base commander testified about the state of negotiations with Fassi and Badeem generally, refusing to go into any detail but stating that, even though they had now been called to a temporary halt in light of the court-martial, the discussions related to a long-term renewal of the lease on the whole base. He, along with Carlson, both testified about the session with Lieutenant Gardner, largely confirming each other's recollection. Paul cross-examined the base commander in connection with Gardner's response to the charge.

"Sir, after you read the charge to Lieutenant Gardner, what did he say to you?"

"He admitted knowing Monsieur Fassi and said he had seen him in the sandy area of the base. He didn't say anything about Monsieur Badeem. All in all, he was very flustered by the charge and just denied it after signing the documents we presented to him."

"Are there any military installations in that part of the base, the area where the bluffs are?"

"No. We may one day use that area, but for now there is no equipment or storage there."

By the time the base commander and Carlson had concluded their testimony, it was mid-afternoon. The prosecution had also called a fellow officer who testified that he had seen Monsieur Fassi and Lieutenant Gardner at the Franco-American Club, but on cross-examination, he could not establish whether he saw them there at the same time or, if so, whether they were talking to each other. After that, Wright stated that he had no other witnesses to call and the prosecution rested. The judge adjourned the proceedings for the day, indicating that the court-martial would reconvene the following morning.

As soon as Paul left the courtroom, he went to the phone exchange and called Lila. He had spoken to her several times after their first conversation subsequent to Michel's death. During the second call, they set a prearranged time to speak each week in the late afternoon. In those conversations, they would report on what was going on in their lives, which fortified them both in the challenges they each faced. This call was no different and ended with them urging each other on and warmly looking forward to the next one. After leaving the phone exchange and having dinner, Paul spent the evening finalizing his opening statement and the order in which he expected to call his witnesses. As the hearing opened at 9:30 a.m. the next day, Paul stepped forward and asked permission to address the jurors.

"Proceed," stated the judge.

"Members of the jury, you have heard the prosecution's case which essentially consists of the incriminating statements of two witnesses, one who claims to have been accosted by Lieutenant Gardner and the other who would have you believe he observed it. You will now hear testimony which will establish what really took place and the actual reason why the witnesses for the prosecution testified as they did. Some of the evidence may not be pleasant to hear, but it will be the truth. You as jurors should certainly not weigh Lieutenant Gardner's testimony more favorably than that of the prosecution's witnesses because he is an officer in the U.S. Navy. At the same time, you must not lean over backward to believe the prosecution's two key witnesses because they represent the monarchy with whom we are negotiating the future of this base. And you will soon see why I emphasize those negotiations. I now wish to call Lieutenant Gardner as my first witness."

After being sworn in and confirming his identity and other basic information, Paul proceeded to ask him about the incident in question.

"Did you see Monsieur Fassi on the day you are accused of molesting him?"

"Yes, I did."

"Will you please describe what you observed?"

"I happened to be heading for a meeting at the communications center, the one near the airstrip. As I was walking there along the back path near the top of one of the bluffs, I suddenly ran into Monsieur Fassi. He seemed to be inspecting the whole bluff area. I was surprised to see him. I had met him in town on a couple of occasions, but I couldn't understand what he was doing on the base all alone. I knew nothing about the negotiations that have now been referred to. I stopped to say hello, and we exchanged a few words."

"Did you shake hands with him?"

"Yes. It's my normal greeting."

"Was he uncomfortable with the handshake?"

"Not that I recall. My father had taught me when I was a youngster to shake hands firmly. He told me it's a sign of manhood. I do recall that Monsieur Fassi shook my hand somewhat limply. I had learned that that was his custom, and I accepted it as such."

"Did you ask him why he was there?"

"He just said he was at a meeting on the base which he was sure I knew about. I said nothing in response. I was curious as to why he was by himself seeming to be studying aspects of the bluff area. He told me he was only taking a break from the meeting. I didn't think much of it and moved on to the communications center. That was it. The whole business about my accosting him is a complete fabrication."

"When you say you had met him in town, when and where was that?"

"Well, I wish I could say it was only at the Franco-American Club, but I can't. I suspect that Monsieur Fassi was counting on my not disclosing where we had both been and seen each other, but I am under oath. We saw each other at one of the town brothels, the one next door to the pharmacy. I met and talked with Monsieur Fassi and Monsieur Badeem there. The women at the brothel were European, not Arab. Even though they themselves are Arabs, they readily told me they preferred coming there."

Fassi leaned over and furiously whispered something in the prosecutor's ear. Wright then rose.

"I object. We have nothing but his word that Monsieurs Fassi and Badeem attended a brothel in Port Lyautey. And what relevance is the location of where the accused says he met them?"

"Your Honor, I will demonstrate the relevance through other witnesses."

"Objection overruled. Counsel, I trust that you will be able to show the relevance as indicated. Otherwise, I will strike that part of the accused's testimony. Proceed."

"Did you tell the base commander about seeing Monsieur Fassi on the bluff?"

"I did. He stated that he was in delicate negotiations with Monsieur Fassi who was representing the monarchy. This explanation was given to me at the time I was called to his office and the charge read to me. I was aghast and terribly upset. It was completely untrue. I had no idea why Fassi would make up such a lie."

"Did you see Monsieur Badeem anywhere in the bluff area when you came upon Monsieur Fassi?"

"No. I didn't see another soul."

"I have no further questions at this time."

Wright rose from his chair, took a look at his notes, and approached the witness stand.

"Lieutenant Gardner, why were you late for the meeting you were on the way to attend?"

"I had been processing some documents in my office and the time got away from me."

"Wasn't the reason you were late because you were diverted by your run-in with Monsieur Fassi?"

Paul decided not to object. He hoped Gardner would effectively deny what was alleged to have taken place.

"If you mean by 'run-in' the thing I'm charged with, the answer is 'no.' There was no homosexual incident. That's a lie. I hate to emphasize it, but I do visit the brothel in town."

"Didn't a fellow officer testify that he had seen both you and Monsieur Fassi at the Franco-American Club, not at any supposed brothel?"

"If I recall the testimony, he didn't say when he saw us there and whether we were talking with each other. I have no memory of ever conferring with Monsieur Fassi at the Franco-American Club. I know I did at the brothel."

Paul was pleased with the firmness of Gardner's response, and he could see that the jury was listening intently. At this point, Wright ended his questioning.

"I wish to call my next witness."

"Proceed."

The petty officer assigned to the courtroom went to the lobby and returned escorting a European-looking woman who was probably in her mid-fifties. Her frumpiness gave the impression of an aging housewife. As she walked down the aisle toward the witness stand, she made a knowing gesture toward Fassi. He looked away instantly and said something to Wright.

Before she reached the witness chair, the prosecutor rose and objected.

"Your Honor, whoever this witness is, I was never given her name or told she would testify. I've had no time to check out whether she is a legitimate witness or what she might say."

Paul responded. "I was not required to give the prosecutor the name of this witness. The local rule only calls on me to provide him with the names of potential military witnesses."

The judge asked both attorneys to step to the bench. Referring to the rule in question, he stated, "I concede that that's the way the rule reads. What I will do is permit the witness to testify on direct. Lieutenant Commander Wright, when the direct is finished, if you need time to prepare for your cross-examination, we will adjourn until the next day."

That was essentially the decision Paul had hoped for. In carefully reading the rules in preparation for trial, he had found a way around the apparent requirement of disclosing all of his witnesses to the prosecution before they testified. Even though the judge's decision would give the other side a chance to prepare for cross-examination, the element of surprise that Paul had planned for was still very much there. Fassi had lost the opportunity to take some secretive action in advance of the trial that might deter the witness from agreeing to testify or alter what she might say on the stand.

Paul addressed the witness as soon as she was seated. "Before I begin, let me ask if you speak English?"

"I do."

The judge administered the oath. "Please raise your right hand. Do you swear that the testimony you are about to give will be the truth, the whole truth, and nothing but the truth, so help you God?"

"Again, I do."

"Please state your name," said Paul.

"Madame Pauline de Rondelier."

"Do you have an occupation?"

"Yes."

"Please state what it is."

"I am the madame of the House of Rondelier."

"And what is that?"

"The House of Rondelier is the finest brothel in Port Lyautey."

The judge and jurors leaned forward in their chairs.

"Do you know Monsieur Fassi?" he asked, pointing toward him.

"I certainly do. He is a client of mine."

"When you say 'client,' what exactly do you mean?"

"He comes to my establishment with some regularity. If there is a particular hostess that he would care to be with, I do my best to arrange it unless she is otherwise engaged. I always try to find the best for my clients. I have many."

She smiled at the jurors. Some of them looked away.

Paul pointed to Lieutenant Gardner. "Do you know this man?"

"Yes, though he only rarely comes—certainly not with the frequency of Monsieur Fassi."

"Does Monsieur Fassi ever come with a male friend?"

"Yes, much of the time he is with Monsieur Badeem. I saw him just before I entered this room. I merely gestured to him as I did to Monsieur Fassi."

"Do you recall any conversations with Lieutenant Gardner other than ones for business purposes?" Paul tried to refer to what goes on at the brothel as discreetly as he could.

"One conversation does stand out in my mind."

"When did that occur?"

"I would say it was a month or two ago."

"Please describe the conversation."

"It stands out because it was so naive, so American, so humorous. Lieutenant Gardner was next to me as I was directing traffic, as we say. I clearly recall his telling me that he was surprised to see so many homosexual men among the Arabs in the medina. I asked what made him think they were homosexuals. He said every time he was in that part of Port Lyautey, he observed Arab men strolling one way or the other holding hands. I laughed very loudly. I told him that when he saw Arab men holding hands, it had nothing to do with their being homosexuals. This was merely an Arab custom, nothing more."

At this point, the prosecutor rose. "Your Honor, I strenuously object to this testimony. It has no relevance to this case and merely demonstrates that the accused knew nothing about local custom."

"If you will permit me to continue," said Paul to the judge, "I will demonstrate its relevance."

"You better demonstrate it quickly, or I'll have it all stricken," stated the judge.

"Madame Rondelier, did anyone overhear this conversation with Lieutenant Gardner?"

"Yes. Monsieurs Fassi and Badeem were sitting together on a nearby couch, and they laughed the same as I did. After Lieutenant Gardner walked away, they were still laughing, and both of them told me how stupid he was. I said he wasn't stupid, just naive. They kept laughing, and I finally left to deal with the needs of several clients."

"Did you hear any other conversation between these two Arab gentlemen?"

"Yes, I did. I soon returned to where they were sitting and stood behind them. Their backs were to me, so they didn't see me. I just listened while the two of them spoke to each other. They were talking in an Arab dialect that I happened to understand. I am good at languages. I have to be because of all the different tongues I deal with. They continued talking feverishly, not knowing I was within hearing distance and, anyway, not thinking anyone would know what they were saying. But I heard it all."

"And what was it they said, as best you can recall?"

"They were talking about the naval base. Monsieur Fassi did most of the talking. He said that the bluff portion of the base away from where the planes land would be extremely valuable for development and the two of them could get it for themselves and sell it off to some wealthy Arab or European investors. Monsieur Fassi urged Monsieur Badeem—through his close contacts with the monarchy—to get him appointed the monarchy's chief negotiator on the future of the base."

"By 'him' do you mean Monsieur Fassi?" Paul interrupted.

"Yes, Monsieur Fassi."

"Okay, go on."

"Monsieur Fassi said that the way to negotiate with the Americans would be to demand, in return for a long-term renewal of the lease, that they give up the bluff portion of the base to the monarchy. He would have himself named as the monarchy's trustee in the documents when the deal was concluded so he could handle the ultimate sale of the land and control the proceeds after the sale. I was so struck by what was being said that I clearly remember it all."

As she was describing the conversation, Paul saw Hadj Radwan, the king's observer, lean forward in his chair and stare at Fassi.

"Did they say any more?"

"No. They just rose and walked out of the room."

"Did you see them again?"

"I have perhaps seen them a few times more, but I had no conversation with them except to arrange hostesses for them."

The afternoon session was nearing the point at which the judge had earlier indicated they would adjourn until the following morning.

"Lieutenant (j.g.) Miner," said the judge, "it is almost four thirty. Do you have any more questions for this witness?"

"I may have more, but I can ask them in the morning before Lieutenant Commander Wright begins his cross-examination."

"Your Honor," said Wright, "I want to be able to hear all of Madame Rondelier's direct testimony so I can properly prepare my cross. I think that was essentially your ruling."

"You're correct. Lieutenant (j.g.) Miner, I am prepared to continue until you finish."

Paul thought for a few seconds. He concluded that he had gotten all the testimony he wanted.

"No further questions, Your Honor."

"Good. Madame Rondelier, you are excused until tomorrow morning at nine thirty, at which time I would appreciate you're being prepared to testify further. The jurors are also excused with the reminder that you are to speak to no one involved in this case. If you are approached by any such person, you are to report it to me. We're adjourned."

As soon as he left the courtroom, Paul raced after Madame Rondelier. He arranged to have dinner with her that evening so he could prepare her for her cross-examination.

"I will see you tonight," she said to him. "I do hope it won't go on all day tomorrow. I have my business to attend to."

As she walked away, Paul thought about whether he should have so readily ended her testimony but decided, all in all, ending it made the most sense. In the event anything came out on cross-examination that he hadn't anticipated, he could try to cover it on redirect.

Madame Rondelier went straight to her bordello. Paul went to the legal department and for the next few hours studied his notes on the day's testimony and prepared for his meeting with Madame Rondellier. After leaving his office, he hurried to the restaurant where they were to meet and waited for her at a table. As time passed, she did not appear. He continued to wait, but still she didn't show. He finally decided to go over to her establishment. When he got there, he asked to see her but was told she had left. He went back to the restaurant, but she was nowhere to be seen. At that point, Paul began to really worry, imagining the worst possible scenarios. But there was nothing more he could do.

When he walked into the courtroom lobby the next morning, there was Madame Rondelier standing by herself. Paul went up to her and told her about his efforts to find her the night before. She shrugged him off, which made him worry even more. He decided to turn his attention to preparing her as best he could for her pending cross-examination and proceeded to do so. She listened but said nothing. Paul left her in the lobby and entered the courtroom. The judge was already there.

"Lieutenant Commander Wright, I assume you are prepared to commence your cross-examination of yesterday's last witness."

"Indeed I am, Your Honor."

At this point, Judge Getters ordered the petty officer to bring in Madame Rondelier. He did so and she proceeded to go directly to the witness stand. After being reminded that she was under oath, the judge instructed the prosecutor to begin his cross-examination.

"Madame Rondelier, did Lieutenant Gardner ask you to testify for him?"

"No."

"Who asked you?"

Pointing to Paul, she replied, "He did."

"Did he come to your establishment to talk to you?"

"No. I had never seen him before. He called me and asked if we could meet at a restaurant in town. He told me who he was. I was a little suspicious, but since we would be at a restaurant where I knew other people, I said I would meet him."

"What did he say to you at the restaurant?"

"He told me about the accusation against Lieutenant Gardner and asked if I knew Monsieur Fassi. I nodded that I did but was reluctant to say any more. He mentioned Lieutenant Gardner asking me about Arab men holding hands. I guess the lieutenant had told him about that. I still hesitated but finally told him what I remembered, which is what I said yesterday."

"Before you said anything to him, didn't Lieutenant (j.g.) Miner refer to the supposed conversation you overheard between Monsieur Fassi and Monsieur Badeem about gaining a portion of the base for themselves?"

"No, not at all. He didn't know about the conversation. He just asked me if I remembered anything else. As I said earlier, it all was very clear in my mind because I was shocked to hear what they were saying. Even so, I wasn't sure I should disclose it, but from what I was told about the accusation, I just decided to. I had kept what I overheard inside me until then. I hadn't told anyone, not even my husband."

Suddenly, Monsieur Fassi yelled out from his seat to Wright. "Please come over here." The prosecutor asked the judge's permission to interrupt his questioning to have a brief word with Fassi. After conferring with him, he resumed the cross-examination.

"Madame Rondelier, when you testified yesterday about that so-called conversation between Monsieur Fassi and Monsieur Badeem, you said that they must have been talking in their own Arab dialect. I suggest to you that you made up that conversation. The only people who speak that dialect come from the village where the two of them grew up. It is a remote place high in the Atlas Mountains near Ouarzazate. To prove it, with the judge's consent, I'm going to have Monsieur Fassi speak to you in that dialect and I want you to translate what he is saying."

Turning to Paul, the judge stated, "Counsel, this is a rather unusual approach to cross-examination, but I'm inclined to permit it."

Paul remained silent.

"Monsieur Fassi is instructed to speak slowly and clearly," stated the judge.

Fassi stepped forward so Madame Rondelier could hear every word he was saying. He began, uttering five or six lines as the witness listened intently. Paul glanced at Hadj Radwan who had a puzzled look on his face, indicating he couldn't understand the dialect Fassi was speaking. When he finished, he smiled and bowed his head slightly as he withdrew to his seat. The prosecutor requested that she translate what Fassi had said.

"Well," she stated, "I know what he said and here it is: 'You are a French bitch. You are no longer welcome in this country. I will make sure that your brothel is closed. I will also see to it that your husband loses his job. You will promptly find that Morocco is not the place for you.'"

"Your Honor," shouted the prosecutor, "I want that testimony stricken. She has made it all up. She doesn't understand that dialect, so she just made up his testimony. It is outrageous to think Monsieur Fassi would say such things. She is surely trying to paint him in the worst possible light because of her testimony yesterday."

Paul rose and approached the bench. "Your Honor, the question here is whether Madame Rondelier correctly translated what Monsieur Fassi said, not whether what he said reflects well on him or not. I should be given the opportunity to demonstrate that she properly translated his words."

Paul had watched Fassi jump from his seat when Madame Rondelier disclosed the conversation she overheard and say something to Wright that could not be overheard. He drew what he hoped was the right conclusion from it. This happened when only those currently in the courtroom were present. Based on his surmise about the whispered conversation with Wright, Paul made his move. He first had to get the judge's approval.

"Sir, you have permitted Monsieur Fassi to render a statement in his dialect in the midst of Madame Rondelier's cross-examination and I raised no objection. I believe I am also entitled to interrupt her testimony so I can be permitted to call a witness who can support the correctness of her translation."

"Will this mean that we'll have to adjourn while you seek out whoever this witness is? Are we going to be involved in a long delay in the court-martial?" asked the judge.

"No, Your Honor. There will be no delay."

"Well," said the judge, "we've already departed from the usual procedures a number of times. I'll permit it once more."

Everyone in the courtroom looked mystified, everyone, that is, except Fassi and the prosecutor who had a sense of what might be coming. Paul had advised the prosecutor that he might well be calling the witness in question and thus to make him available.

"Your Honor, I call Monsieur Badeem as a hostile witness."

As Badeem was being summoned from the lobby and led down the aisle, Fassi attempted to catch his eye but Badeem's view of Fassi was inadvertently blocked by the prosecutor. Badeem took the witness stand as Madame Rondelier passed him on her way to the lobby. Paul immediately stepped into a position in front of Badeem so he couldn't see Fassi's face.

"Your Honor, I request that the witness be sworn in again, even though he has previously testified," stated Paul.

The judge administered the oath a second time. Realizing that Badeem might quickly grasp what effect his translation might have, Paul decided to have the court reporter read one word at a time after which Badeem would be called upon to translate each word before the court reporter read the next one.

Paul began. "Please read the first word of the most recent testimony."

The court reporter looked at his shorthand transcription while at the same time placing his earphones on so he could listen to the word as he had recorded it. He then spoke the word out loud, stating it as phonetically as he could.

"Okay, Monsieur Badeem, please translate that word in English."

Badeem looked haplessly in the direction of Fassi, but Paul made sure his view continued to be blocked. He finally decided that the word he was being asked to translate seemed harmless, so he said it. "You."

"Next," said Paul.

The court reporter stated the next word.

This one, too, seemed harmless. "are."

"Next."

Badeem continued in the same mode. "a."

"Next."

"French."

At this point, the prosecutor jumped to his feet. "Your Honor—"

Before he could say anything more, the judge firmly stopped him.

"You are to say nothing until this witness finishes his testimony."

Wright sat down in grim silence.

"Next."

The court reporter knew from Madame Rondelier's translation what the next word meant. After pronouncing it as clearly as possible, Badeem looked at the judge and asked if the word could be repeated.

"Say the word again as loud and clear as you can," instructed the judge. The court reporter said it again.

"I apologize for saying so, but that word means 'bitch.'" Thinking his next comment would be helpful to Fassi, he went on. "I also apologize for telling you that whoever said it must have been referring to Madame Rondelier." He chuckled.

The judge stated, "Counsel, I don't think it will be necessary for you to continue with this witness. The jurors should be capable of weighing the validity of the matter at issue without more. The witness is excused."

Badeem rose from the witness chair and jauntily strode down the aisle, nodding at Fassi with a certain playful expression on his face. Fassi turned his face away.

"Lieutenant Commander Wright, do you wish to continue your cross-examination of Madame Rondelier?"

"No, Your Honor. I am finished."

"Lieutenant (j.g.) Miner, do you have any further witnesses?"

"I do, Your Honor. I call Monsieur Fassi as a hostile witness."

"I object," said the prosecutor. "He has already had an opportunity to cross-examine Monsieur Fassi."

"I believe I am entitled to question him in light of Monsieur Badeem's testimony, which further raises the question of Monsieur Fassi's credibility," said Paul.

"The objection is overruled. Monsieur Fassi will take the stand."

Wright turned to Fassi and pointed. "You'll have to go there," he said.

Fassi slowly walked to the witness box, his stride this time reflecting an air of fear.

"Your Honor, I also wish to have this witness sworn in again."

Judge Getters agreed and swore in the witness once more.

"Monsieur Fassi, when you saw Lieutenant Gardner on the bluff overlooking the ocean on the day in question, where did you think he was going before he stopped to talk with you?"

"I didn't know."

"Weren't you afraid that he might have some role in the negotiations that you were involved in at the base?"

"Again, I didn't know. He wasn't at the meeting with the base commander and his staff."

"But that didn't mean he wasn't involved. And didn't that make you worry about his seeing you there on the bluff? You thought he might tell the base commander you were there."

Before Fassi could answer, the prosecutor objected. "Your Honor, there is no basis for the questions counsel is asking. He is making things up."

"Lieutenant (j.g.) Miner, do you have a response?"

"Your Honor, in light of the prior testimony, I think I'm entitled to explore along the line I am on."

The judge eased back in his chair. He brought himself forward and looked straight at the prosecutor. "Your objection is overruled. We will see where this leads. If it goes nowhere, the testimony will be stricken." Turning to Fassi, the judge firmly stated, "Answer the question."

Fassi appeared uneasy. "I was just out for a walk."

Paul kept at it. "Weren't you worried that Lieutenant Gardner might grasp why you were really on the bluff?"

"Of course not," Fassi responded with as much determination as he could muster.

"And when Lieutenant Gardner left you on the bluff, didn't you fear that he would soon tell the base commander that you were there?"

"Of course not," he replied, again in the same manner.

"And didn't you remember the question that Lieutenant Gardner asked Madame Rondelier about whether Arab men holding hands meant they were homosexuals, the one that you and Monsieur Badeem laughed about?"

This time, Fassi merely shook his head sideways.

"I will take that as a 'no,' a rather weak one," stated Paul.

He then asked Fassi, "And in a fit of worry about Lieutenant Gardner disclosing what you were really doing on the bluff, didn't his question to Madame Rondelier come to mind? And didn't it give you the idea of accusing him of a homosexual act against you to deflect any attention from what he might report to the base commander?"

"No, no, no!" Fassi shouted. Turning to Wright, he yelled, "Aren't you going to stop him? I need you to stop him."

At this point, the judge, *sua sponte*, inserted himself with his own question. "And why do you need Lieutenant Wright to stop him?"

"Because, because . . ."

Concentrating his glare directly into Fassi's eyes, the judge directed his next question. "Is it because Lieutenant (j.g.) Miner has unearthed why you really were on the bluff?"

As the judge continued his unflinching focus, Fassi sensed the U.S. military closing in on him. "I, I . . ." He stopped and just sat there gripping the sides of the chair.

"We will take a brief recess." Pointing at Hadj Radwan, the judge said, "Sir, may I ask you to step forward and join me outside?" Radwan moved to the platform where the judge was now standing. The two of them walked out a side door together.

Within fifteen minutes, the judge was back with two petty officers at his side. Hadj Radwan was not with him. Everyone rose and stayed standing. "Counsel, please step forward." They both approached the bench, but before reaching it, the judge held up his hands, signaling them to stop. "I am directing my statement to counsel, but it is also for the others in this courtroom. As a result of the testimony that has come forth, I along with Hadj Radwan, the King of Morocco's observer at these proceedings, have conferred with the base commander during the recess. With the commander's authorization, I am ordering these petty officers to take Monsieur Fassi and Monsieur Badeem into immediate custody. Monsieur Radwan will report the conclusions he has drawn from the testimony in this court-martial to the king and his legal minister. Upon written and signed instructions from the authorized Moroccan authorities, Monsieur Fassi and Monsieur Badeem will be delivered into the hands of the appropriate officers of the monarchy. We will reconvene at the usual hour tomorrow morning."

By this time, one of the petty officers had swiftly moved to where Fassi was standing and placed handcuffs on him while the other entered the lobby and did the same to Badeem. They were taken directly to the brig.

That evening, Paul and Gardner had dinner together at Paul's favorite restaurant in town. They invited Madame Rondelier to join them, and this time she actually appeared. Paul had gotten permission from the judge to take Gardner with him on the condition that he would be responsible for returning him to his confinement on the base. The jury had not been instructed by the judge to deliberate on a verdict as yet, and Gardner would not know until the following morning if he would be released from the restrictions imposed on him. Accordingly, there was no celebration at dinner, just a sense of relief. After a toast of gratitude by Gardner to Paul and thanks to Madame Rondelier for testifying, the three of them discussed the highlights of the trial during dinner. In the midst of their discussion, Paul decided to pose a question to Madame Rondelier that he had hesitated to ask until after the comfort of Moroccan wine and good French cooking had worked to ease any barriers she may have erected to hide behind.

"Can you please tell me," Paul said as gently as he could, "now that you no longer have the burden of testifying at the court-martial, where you were last night when I was desperately looking for you?"

"Are you sure you want to know?"

"Yes, of course. I was terribly worried for your safety. I was afraid Fassi would either prevent your testimony or force you to change it."

"You shouldn't have worried. I know my way around. I decided to go with my husband to the one place in town where I was quite certain no one would be able to find us. I, too, was afraid of what Fassi might try to do."

"And where may I ask was that?"

"Well, I am a good Catholic woman, but I thought Fassi might look for me at our church if I wasn't at my home."

"So where did you go?"

"I decided we should go to the synagogue in the mellah. I know the rabbi quite well, and I was sure he would hide us there. And he did. He provided us with a bed in the room behind where he prays. Fortunately he has not left for Israel yet. Most of his parishioners—that's what I call them—have already gone. I knew that would be the last place Fassi would think to look for us. The next day after we left the synagogue, my husband drove me to the base in time for me to meet you in the lobby outside the courtroom."

The jaws of both Paul and Gardner dropped. "I should have known you had the cleverness to protect yourself," said Paul.

"In my business, you have to know every avenue."

The following morning, the usual assemblage, including a handcuffed Fassi and Badeem, stood up as the judge entered the courtroom.

"Be seated. I have in my hand a proclamation that was delivered to the base commander late last night. It has been translated into English, so before I enter my ruling in this case, I think it is important for me to read it to you. It states as follows: 'Mohammed II, Supreme Ruler of the Kingdom of Morocco, proclaims and conveys to you His sincerest apologies for the fraudulent and reprehensible misconduct of Hassan Fassi and Samir Badeem who, pursuant to His Majesty's appointment for the purpose of legitimate discussions with senior military officers of the United States Navy in connection with the future of the U.S. Naval Air Station at Port Lyautey, advanced their own despicable and odious ends without the knowledge or consent of His Majesty. In view thereof and as a gesture of friendship to the American people, the King, speaking from His royal throne and through the divine guidance of Allah, hereby grants and conveys to the United States Navy a 10-year extension of the current lease on the aforesaid Air Station, including its associated communications sites at Sidi Yahia and Sidi Buchnadel, on the same terms as presently exist. The specific provisions of the lease, which shall reflect this proclamation, will be concluded in writing by and between able and honorable appointees of His Majesty and those appointed representatives of the Naval Air Station. His Majesty, on behalf of the Moroccan people and as their King, begs the forgiveness of all who have been afflicted by the malfeasance of Hassan Fassi and Samir Badeem and assures those so afflicted that He shall certainly impose on these two contemptible miscreants the most severe instrument of corrective justice that is within His power.'"

Judge Getters then stated, "The proclamation concludes with the signature of the king and the royal seal of the Moroccan monarchy. It further proclaims that copies of it shall be posted at the entryway of the principal government center in every city and village throughout the land."

The judge turned to counsel. "Given the testimony that has come before this court, I do not consider it necessary for either of you to make a closing argument. Nor do I consider it necessary to take up any further time of the jurors in this case, though I do wish to thank them for their careful and dutiful attention to the testimony as presented. Accordingly, I hereby direct a verdict of not guilty in favor of Lt. Robert Gardner and further order that he be freed from his confinement and wholly reinstated to his rank as a full lieutenant in the U.S. Navy. In keeping with the motion of his counsel, Lieutenant Junior Grade Paul Miner, and pursuant to my order granting said motion, the testimony in these proceedings, and all other relevant aspects thereof shall remain permanently sealed, and in no way shall any of it adversely affect or bring disrepute to or on the military record of Lieutenant Robert Gardner. These proceedings are closed."

Chapter 13

After shaking hands firmly with Lieutenant Gardner, Paul headed for his room. He was exhilarated by the outcome but completely exhausted. He didn't even have the energy to call Lila. After a long rest and a late-afternoon meal, however, he walked to the phone exchange and dialed her number. Her mother answered and, still uncertain of how she might react to his voice, he abruptly hung up. While he stood there in the exchange wondering what to do next, the telephone operator asked if he was Paul Miner.

After he nodded yes, he said, "Sir, you have a call."

He picked up the phone and heard Lila's voice. "Did you just call me?" she asked. After telling her he had, she went on. "I somehow sensed it was you. I was standing right there when my mother answered and she told me someone had hung up on her. She walked out of the room, and I immediately tried the number at the base. How are you? Is the case over? Have you won?"

"It is over, and we have won," he happily responded.

"How wonderful! I want to hear all about it."

"Can I come to see you in Tangier?"

"I no longer see why not. I think about you so much of the time. We could even go away together."

"Yes, yes, I will be with you soon."

Paul told her a bit about the trial and arranged to meet her three days hence. He wanted to drive there immediately but knew that he would have things to attend to at his office that had piled up while he was consumed by the Gardner trial. Notwithstanding that the case's outcome had brought embarrassment to Carlson, he was still Paul's commanding officer, and he wanted to iron out his relations with him, even if Carlson was the one who should be doing the ironing. Were he to take off for Tangier promptly after the trial, Carlson would feel belittled. Besides, his tour of duty was within days of ending.

When he arrived at the legal department the following morning, Paul found a note on his desk. It was from Carlson. "Please drop into my office when you have a chance."

Paul had other thoughts going through his head, but at some point, he decided he couldn't put off Carlson's request any longer. He straightened his tie and proceeded down the hall. "May I come in . . . sir?"

"Come in, come in." The welcoming sound of his voice was rather surprising to Paul. For some reason, it reminded him of Nikita Novikov's greeting, absent any offering from a carafe of vodka. "I'm sure everyone has told you what a splendid job you did, but I just wanted to add my two-cents' worth. I learned from the ordeal, too, and I'm anxious for you to know that."

Having praised Paul, he went on to address the matter he had really called him in for. "There's something I want you to think about. I know it's a little late, since your tour of duty is about to end. I'd like you to consider extending your service for a year and continue trying cases here. I can get approval for it. We need you a great deal, and you will immediately be promoted to full lieutenant."

Paul was pleased with Carlson's words, stated without repetition, but merely thanked him and said he'd have to think about it. What he didn't want to say was that he had no intention of extending his military commitment. His intentions were completely otherwise. They had crystallized early that morning before coming to work.

He had watched the sun rising in the east just after he woke up. He didn't dream during the night, at least not that he remembered, but he was in a reminiscent and dreamy mood when he awoke. He ensconced himself in the one comfortable chair the navy had provided in his room and closed his eyes. He found himself envisioning aspects of the trial, the faces of the principal characters—their smiles, their angers, their movements—as though out of a novel—but what constantly came into view was the figure of Lila, first as he saw her in Rabat at the train station and then upon hearing her lilting voice over the phone the day before when she asked if he had won. He began to dwell on his future with her. He saw himself upon his release from the navy getting into his MG and driving to Tangier rather than returning to his family in America. Lila would be waiting for him and they would board the ferry for Gibraltar. Over the next several months, they would travel throughout Europe, from the south of Spain to Madrid, then over the Pyrenees and onward to Paris and from there north to Scandinavia. They would secretly marry at some point and live out their lives happily ever after. Paul would prove Tolstoy wrong; he and his Anna Karenina would last for a lifetime.

These were the images in Paul's mind upon arriving at work that morning and as he later met with Carlson. The next day, he informed Carlson of his decision not to extend his service requirement. Carlson thereupon instructed him to finish meeting with the other lawyers in the office who would be taking over his workload. That night, his last, he finally responded to an open invitation from Madame Novikov, whom he had not seen for some time in light of his involvement in the Gardner case and in view of his having spent whatever free time he had with Lila. He even drank a little vodka as a toast to their friendship. He alluded to his relationship with Lila hoping Madame Novikov would ask more, but she said nothing. At the end of the evening, they warmly embraced, and he assured her that one day they would see each other again. He drove back to the base in the dark, feeling giddy from the continuing shots of vodka, and descended into bed.

At some point, he began to dream. *He was driving to Tangier when, not unlike what happened on the way to Rabat, the car's engine started to sputter and, as he pulled over to the side of the road it died. He got out and raised the hood. He played around with the spark plugs, checked the oil, and then tried to start the engine. Nothing happened. He got out again and looked in both directions. No cars in sight. The Atlantic Ocean was in the distance to his left, and there was nothing but sub-desert to his right.*

All at once, two men emerged out of nowhere. They were olive-skinned with white beards. They peered at Paul and began speaking Hebrew. Paul recited the Shema, and the two men, hearing the prayer, moved in his direction, warmly embraced him, and immediately fixed the car. They then said their own Hebrew prayer, assuming Paul would understand, which he didn't, and disappeared into the sub-desert. Paul got back in his car, whose motor was now humming. Suddenly, another car approached and pulled up in front of him, blocking his departure. Out of the car emerged his parents.

His father firmly stepped to the driver's side of the car. His mother opened the door on the other side and sat next to him.

"Where do you think you're going?" his father asserted.

"Er . . . I guess I didn't tell you. I'm not coming home. I'm going to Tangier to be with Lila, the woman I love. I expect we will be married soon."

"Is this Lila Jewish?"

"Er . . . no."

"What is she?"

"She's Russian Orthodox."

"Have you gone mad?"

"We've never discussed religion much. She knows I'm Jewish. She still loves me."

"Do you realize what a tragedy this is for your mother and me? You are inflicting terrible pain on us."

Paul did not respond immediately. He then answered respectfully.

"But I thought this is what you wanted. You turned me into Paul after first being Saul. You sent me to the best schools where I would blend into the Christian world. You wanted me to be accepted."

"Not at the price of leaving us, of bringing misery to us, of going away from the religion you were born into," pleaded his mother.

"You will like her," he urged. "She comes from Russian aristocratic stock. And she will like you."

"Russian aristocratic stock. Do you know how those people treated your people?"

"She is not that way. They have suffered too."

"If you have children, they will not be Jewish. She is not Jewish. The children will be raised Russian Orthodox. God help us."

The nightmare that began as a dream suddenly ended. Paul rose up from his pillow. It was covered with sweat. His nightshirt was drenched in perspiration. He quickly got out of bed and showered. The sun was again rising in the east as Paul gazed out the window. He stumbled to the chair where he had sat two mornings before. He bent over with his elbows on his knees and his hands over his eyes. He sat there shuttering for the next ten minutes. Then he rose and made his way over to his desk. He pulled out a piece of stationery from the drawer, turned on the light so he could see as clearly as possible, and took up his pen.

My Dearest Lila,

This is very hard for me to write. I expected to be leaving shortly to come to you but I find that I cannot. No one is standing in my way except what is going on inside of me. There are differences between us that neither of us has dwelled on, at least to each other. I am a Jew. You are Russian Orthodox. We are from different worlds which will affect us more and more as we live together and raise children.

I have also come to better appreciate the impact that Michel's death is having on you. Your willingness to come with me, to run off with me, may well be more an expression of what you are going through than any separate feelings for me. I would like it to be otherwise, but I'm afraid I will be getting you, as we say, on the rebound. I know I am at least your friend, and as your friend I must speak honestly to you.

I wish I had the courage to say all this in front of you, but I do not. Instead, I will fold this letter and place it in an envelope addressed to you. When you receive it, I will have boarded the plane and be flying back to America, back to my home where I belong. Once you have made your way through your present tragedy, you will realize that what I have said and done here are best for both of us.

Love,

Paul

Epilogue

I met Saul in later life. We became good friends. We would meet for lunch at least once a week, and he would tell me stories about his younger years, particularly about his experience in the U.S. Navy. It wasn't that usual for a Jew to be an officer in the navy then, even if one didn't intend to make a career of it. Of course, there was Admiral Rickover, but he was a real exception. Anyway, I would listen intently as Saul told parts of his story at each lunch. I took copious notes, but I never interrupted him with questions. I was too intent on hearing him out. As a writer myself, I was unsure whether the stories were completely true or whether he fictionalized some of it as he went along.

The last lunch we had was several months ago, just before he became seriously ill. He was only up to answering a few questions at that lunch, probably because he wasn't feeling well, so I did most of the talking. I wanted to know something more about the people he was so close to over fifty years ago.

As soon as we sat down, I asked if "Paul" was the real first name he used as a young man, and he assured me it was. At the previous lunch the week before, he had finished telling me the long story about his time in Morocco, referring to a letter he had written to a woman he called "Lila."

"I assume Paul actually sent that letter," I said. "Or maybe I should say you, Saul, actually send that letter."

"He did, which is to say 'I did,'" Saul replied. "I sent the letter, and I did come home, just as I said I would."

"Was Lila her real first name?"

"Yes, it really was, at least back then."

"I don't understand. Did she change her name later?"

Saul didn't respond. He just shrugged, as if to say it was something he had no control over.

"Well, let me ask this. Did you ever have contact with her again?"

"Not directly," Saul finally said. "Madame Novikov, whose real last name was Lufshin, and I would exchange letters from time to time, and we were together on the one occasion she came to America."

"Did she tell you what happened to Lila?"

"In her letters, she would occasionally mention Lila. She wrote in one letter that Lila had married again, a man from a Russian family in Tangier. Then later she wrote me about Lila's children. When I saw her on her visit here, she said Lila had divorced her husband and married another man."

"Another Russian, I suppose?"

Saul said nothing in reply.

"Another Russian, I suppose?" I repeated.

Saul just remained silent for a while. Then he spoke. "She married a man who lived in Paris, and she moved there."

"Did she tell you anything about him? I assume he was a Frenchman."

"Well, sort of."

"Meaning what?"

Saul seemed unable to get it out.

"You don't have to tell me if you don't want to."

At last he answered. "An observant Jew living in Paris."

"A Jew! My god! Tell me more."

"She converted to Judaism."

"She what!" I exclaimed.

"You heard me."

"Amazing. Anything else?"

"She changed her name. She adopted a Hebrew name, Leila Bat-Chayim," he sputtered.

"I can see how hard this is for you," I said, speaking softly. "Why didn't you ask her to convert back then? Your family might have accepted her."

"It never occurred to me. It was the 1950s, not today. A Russian aristocrat converting to Judaism? Any Christian converting to Judaism? It never crossed my mind."

He went on, regaining a firmness in his voice. "Yes, I once tried to be Paul rather than Saul, but that passed some time ago. I am no longer what I am not. I am what I am. I am Saul! I am Saul!"

He died soon thereafter.

Edwards Brothers, Inc.
Thorofare, NJ USA
May 12, 2011